THE ADVENTURES OF ROBIN HOOD

COLLECTED AND RETOLD BY

ROGER LANCELYN GREEN

ILLUSTRATED BY ARTHUR HALL

Robin Hood is here again: all his merry thieves
Hear a ghostly bugle-note shivering through the leaves ...
The dead are coming back again, the years are rolled away
In Sherwood, in Sherwood, about the break of day.

ALFRED NOYES

PUFFIN BOOKS

PUFFIN BOOKS

Published by the Penguin Group
Penguin Books Ltd, 27 Wrights Lane, London W8 5TZ, England
Penguin Books USA Inc., 375 Hudson Street, New York, New York 10014, USA
Penguin Books Australia Ltd, Ringwood, Victoria, Australia
Penguin Books Canada Ltd, 10 Alcorn Avenue, Toronto, Ontario, Canada M4V 3B2
Penguin Books (NZ) Ltd, 182–190 Wairau Road, Auckland 10, New Zealand

Penguin Books Ltd, Registered Offices: Harmondsworth, Middlesex, England

First published 1956
13 15 17 19 20 18 16 14 12

Copyright © Roger Lancelyn Green, 1956
All rights reserved

Printed in England by Clays Ltd, St Ives plc
Set in Monotype Baskerville

To
'BUSS'
(Miss A. L. Mansfield)
in memory of ROBIN HOOD
and many other
end-of-term plays
at Knockaloe, Poulton,
and Lane End

CONTENTS

CONTENTS

LIST OF ILLUSTRATIONS

AUTHOR'S NOTE

AS TO THE SOURCES FROM WHICH HIS MATERIAL IS DERIVED

To retell the adventures of Robin Hood is a very different matter from writing of King Arthur and his Knights. The Arthurian poems and romances, even if we take Malory as the latest, would fill a bookcase – and in that bookcase we would find some of the great literature of the world, in several languages.

Robin Hood had no Malory, and he has had few poets. A late medieval metrical romance, *A Lytell Geste of Robyn Hode:* a collection of Ballads most of which are the merest doggerel and some of which may be as late as the eighteenth century; a prose rendering of several of the Ballads, and two plays by Anthony Munday, a contemporary of Shakespeare, called *The Downfall of Robert Earl of Huntingdon* and *The Death of Robert Earl of Huntingdon* constitute nearly all that we may call the original Robin Hood Literature. If we add to this several short scraps of medieval folk-plays which merely follow extant ballads, a brief appearance in Robert Greene's play *George-a-Greene the Pinner of Wakefield* and its exactly parallel prose romance, and a rather fuller appearance in Ben Jonson's unfinished pastoral play *The Sad Shepherd*, our sources are complete.

It was only after the ballads, romances, and plays were collected and reprinted by Joseph Ritson at the end of the eighteenth century that Robin Hood found his way into real literature. Even so he found his best expression as a minor character, as all readers of *Ivanhoe* will agree. The majority of the ballads, with a glance at the dramatic background, gave Thomas Love Peacock the outline for the best prose story of Robin Hood yet written, his *Maid Marian* (1822), and the same sources (to which Peacock and Scott also lent something) produced Tennyson's play of *The Foresters* (1881) – a pleasant re-arrangement of the old materials, but of no special merit either as poetry or as drama. It was left for the twentieth century to give us the finest poetic play yet written with Robin as hero, Alfred Noyes's *Robin Hood* (1926 – acted the same year).

There have, of course, been many other minor contributions made to the literature of Robin Hood in the form of plays, operas and adventure stories. But by far the largest number of books about him during the last hundred years consist of various forms of retellings of the old legends – none of which has found a permanent place on the shelf reserved for *The Blue Fairy Book*, *The Heroes* and *Tanglewood Tales*.

My book is based on authority throughout – but that authority has not stopped short with Munday or the Ballads. They have been the main basis of my fabric, but in certain places I have sought the aid of later, literary sources – Noyes and Tennyson as well as Peacock and Scott or Jonson and Greene. I have used all my sources mainly for the outline of the tales, though the dialogue wherever possible is adapted from the ballads – occasionally from the earlier plays, in a few instances from Peacock, and in one obvious instance from Scott.

My first four chapters show perhaps the most varied example of this method of literary mosaic. Chapters 5 to 15 follow almost entirely the *Lytell Geste* and the Ballads, but with selection and a certain amount of conflation and regrouping. Chapter 16 uses two scenes of *George-a-Greene*; Chapter 17 combines a ballad with a chapter of Peacock; Chapter 18 is based on *The Sad Shepherd* (but with my own ending, since that made by F. G. Waldron in the eighteenth century seemed inadequate: the final song alone is Waldron's); Chapter 19 combines two ballads; Chapter 20 selects from *Ivanhoe*, with slight variations to fit my general scheme; 21 is mainly ballad, but here all the authorities converge – one can find lines in the various descriptions of this same incident which are almost identical in Scott, Peacock, Tennyson and Noyes; 22 uses the ballad of 'Robin Hood and the Monk', perhaps the finest of all the ballads regarded as poetry, and an incident from Noyes; while the two final chapters are almost pure ballad, the Death of Robin touching the only note of pathos or tragedy in all the older literature of the subject. Prologue and Epilogue follow ballads also, the second but distantly and with licence. The songs are from Peacock, Tennyson, and medieval sources.

As for the setting I have followed most writers and traditions in choosing the reign of Richard I: but the history, it must be remembered, is *legendary* history, and I have not felt that detailed accuracy in background would help the story. The ballads pay no attention whatever to historical setting, some placing Robin in the reign of Richard I, others in that of one of the Edwards, some even in the time of Henry VIII. Geography too has no place in ballad literature: Robin can flee from Nottingham in the morning, on foot, and find himself in Lancashire the same afternoon, while no ballad writer troubles to wonder why the Bishop of Hereford should be in Sherwood Forest. I have amended some of the grosser errors, just as I have reduced some of Robin's record shots with bow and arrow to within sight at least of probability.

'Many talk of Robin Hood who never shot with his bow,' runs the old saying: I have at least dwelt with him in the Sherwood Forest of romance, and brought back I trust a true report of his life and doings there. For Robin Hood's is a story that can never die, nor cease to fire the imagination. Like the old fairytales it must be told and told again – for like them it is touched with enchantment and few of us can fail to come under its spell –

> *Calling as he used to call, faint and far away,*
> *In Sherwood, in Sherwood, about the break of day.*

ROGER LANCELYN GREEN

Raigne of King Richard the First . . .

In this time were many Robbers and Out-
lawes, among the which, Robert Hood, *and*
little John, *renowned Theeves, continued in*
woods, dispoyling and robbing the goods of the
rich. They killed none but such as would in-
vade them or by resistance to their owne
defence.

The said Robert *intertained an hundred*
tall men, and good archers with such spoiles
and thefts as he got, upon whom foure hundred
(were they never so strong) durst not give the
onset. Hee suffered no woman to be oppressed,
violated or otherwise molested: poore mens
goods hee spared, aboundantlie relieving them
with that which by thefte he got from Abbeys
and the houses of rich Carles: whom Maior
blameth for his rapine and theft but of all
theeves hee affirmeth him to bee the Prince:
and the most gentle Theefe. . . .

STOW: ANNALS OF ENGLAND, 1580

THE BIRTH OF ROBERT FITZOOTH

> *And mony ane sings o' grass, o' grass,*
> *And mony ane sings o' corn,*
> *And mony ane sings o' Robin Hood*
> *Kens little where he was born.*
>
> *It wasna in the ha', the ha',*
> *Nor in the painted bower;*
> *But it was in the gude green-wood,*
> *Amang the lily-flower.*
>
> BALLAD: *The Birth of Robin Hood*

ALTHOUGH it was a hundred years since the Battle of
Hastings, there was no real peace in England. William
the Conqueror had divided the country amongst his followers, only in special cases leaving the old Saxon
Thanes the ownership of even a small part of what had
once been their properties. Often the new Norman earls
and barons and knights, and their sons and grandsons
also, treated the Saxons as mere slaves – serfs to till the
land for them and follow them in war – serfs with no
rights of their own and no chance of real justice.

England was still an 'occupied' country in the twelfth
century, and although there were no big outbreaks after
the death of Hereward the Wake, there were many small
'underground movements', and in every forest there
were outlaws and gangs of robbers. These forests were
the property of the king, and the penalties for killing the
king's deer were cruel and barbarous.

No wonder that in the year 1160 there was little
friendship between Saxon and Norman: no wonder Sir

George Gamwell of Gamwell Hall in Nottinghamshire, a Saxon knight holding the scarred remnant of his ancestors' lands, did not encourage young William Fitzooth, son of the Baron of Kyme, when he came wooing his daughter Joanna.

Sir George was short-tempered and fierce, a bitter man who could never forget his wrongs, nor forgive the Normans whose fathers and grandfathers had wronged him.

As it happened, young William Fitzooth had a Saxon mother and a Saxon grandmother, and was already beginning to feel that he was neither Norman nor Saxon, but British – and that the way to find contentment and security for the country was by justice and not by cruelty.

But Sir George would not listen to William, and forbade him ever to enter his house again. Nor would he listen to his daughter, but ordered her as fiercely to keep to her rooms and have no more dealings with the accursed Norman.

Joanna went weeping away: but she did not obey her father. That night William Fitzooth stood beneath her window, and they swore to be faithful to one another for ever. And not long after, though Sir George had no idea of it, these two were married in secret, meeting like Romeo and Juliet at a nearby chapel.

Then William visited Joanna night by night, climbing perilously to her window in the darkness, and leaving in haste before the daylight came.

Spring turned into Summer, and William was called away for several months to follow his father to London on the king's business. When he returned to Gamwell, a messenger brought him in secret a letter from Joanna.

'I am in sore trouble,' she wrote, 'for, though I keep my bed and fain to be ill, my father will soon know what has chanced between us – and then his fury will be terrible. If he catches you, he will certainly hang you – and I do not know what he will do to me, or to our child when it is born. So come to me quickly, dear William, and carry me away, for I am in constant fear until I feel your strong arms around me.'

Then William called to him three of his most faithful followers, and led them swiftly into Sherwood Forest, where they made their camp not far from Gamwell: for he knew that when Sir George missed his daughter he would suspect him, and seek for her first at Kyme.

When the sun had set, William and his men came silently and stealthily to Gamwell Hall, made their way into the garden, and stood beneath Joanna's window.

She was waiting for them, all ready to flee away, and leapt bravely from the window into the great red cloak which the four held for her. Then William took her in his arms, and carried her slowly and tenderly away from Gamwell and out into the silent forest where the green leaves shimmered in the moonlight and the hoot of an owl or the bark of a fox were the only sounds in the stillness.

When night was gone and the sun shone out, Sir George woke suddenly, and called loudly for his retainers.

'Where is my daughter?' he cried. 'She usually comes to see me at this time in the morning – and there is no sign of her! I dreamt a terrible dream about her – God grant it never comes true! – for I thought that I saw her drowned in the salt sea . . . But look here! If she's been stolen away, or if any harm has come to her – I'll hang the lot of you!'

Then there was fear and commotion at Gamwell Hall, servants running hither and thither, men buckling on

their swords, foresters stringing their bows and seeing to
their arrows.

Sir George came storming through the midst of them,
shouting for his horse and threatening to hang everyone
on the spot unless they found his daughter.

'Well, young Robin, may you be true to the soil of England and
bring help to the down-trodden all your days!'

At last the chief huntsman came with two of his
hounds on a leash, and the whole party set forth into
Sherwood Forest following the trail of William Fitzooth.

And later that day they came suddenly upon Joanna,
sitting in her woodland bower, and nursing her baby
son.

Then Sir George sprang to earth with drawn sword,
swearing dreadful things. But when Joanna smiled up at
him and placed his little grandson in his arms, he

dropped the sword and kissed the child tenderly, exclaiming:

'By God, I'd like to hang your father – but your mother's dear to me still, in spite of everything. . . . Well, well, you're my grandson sure enough, and it would be little kindness on my part to begin by killing your father. Joanna, where is this villain?'

Then William Fitzooth came out from behind a tree and knelt before Sir George, begging his forgiveness and promising to be a special friend to all Saxons for his sweet wife's sake, and for the sake of his little son who himself was more than half a Saxon.

'Well, well,' said Sir George. 'All shall be forgiven and forgotten. And as for this young person – what do you say his name is? Robert? . . . Well, young Robin, born in the good green-wood, and no stately hall or painted bower; may you be true to the soil of England and bring help to the down-trodden all your days!'

CHAPTER ONE

THE GOOD SPIRIT OF SHERWOOD

Sherwood in the twilight, is Robin Hood awake?
Grey and ghostly shadows are gliding through the brake,
Shadows of the dappled deer, dreaming of the morn,
Dreaming of a shadowy man that winds a shadowy horn.

ALFRED NOYES: *Sherwood (1903)*

KING RICHARD THE FIRST, Richard Cœur de Lion, came to the throne in 1189 – and very soon left his throne empty when he set off on the Crusade to free Jerusalem from the Saracens. He was summoned home by the news of trouble and rebellion – but was captured on the way and shut up in a prison – no one knew where – and in England few believed that he would ever return.

When he went away, Richard left the Bishop of Ely to rule for him, but very soon the King's wicked brother, Prince John, accused the Bishop of treason, made him fly for his life, and himself became ruler of the country.

John was a cruel, merciless man, and most of his followers were as bad as he. They needed money, and he needed money: the easiest way of getting it was to accuse some wealthy man of treason or law-breaking, make him an outlaw – and seize his house or castle and all his goods. For an outlaw could own nothing, and anyone who killed him would be rewarded.

When Prince John had seized a man's lands he would usually put one of his own followers in his place – provided he paid him large sums of money. Prince John's followers did not mind how they came by this money: for them the easiest way was to take it from the small farmers, the peasants and even from the serfs. And not only Prince John's upstart knights and squires did this, but many also of the Bishops and Abbots who were either in league with him, or greedy for their own good like the worst of the nobles and barons.

Many a Sheriff, too, was appointed to keep order and administer justice in the towns and counties by Prince John – provided he paid well for the honour: and of course he had also to force the money from someone weaker than himself, and obey Prince John however cruel and unjust his orders might be.

Such a one was the Sheriff of Nottingham, the little town on the edge of Sherwood Forest, and when Prince John came and set up his Court there for a time, he was naturally most eager to show his loyalty and zeal.

One evening he and his men came upon a serf who had killed a deer. Without a thought of pity, the Sheriff ordered the poor man's cottage to be searched for money, and when none was found, had it burnt to the ground.

Then the wretched serf was brought before him.

'You know the Forest Laws,' said the Sheriff grimly. 'All right, my men: one of you heat the irons quickly. Blind him, and turn him loose!'

'No, no! Not that!' shrieked the man. 'Anything but that! Kill me straightaway! If you blind me, God will repay you! Mercy! Mercy!'

Prince John had ridden out to see the Sheriff at work, and at this moment he joined the little group round the glowing embers of the cottage.

'What night-jar have we here?' he asked carelessly. 'Surely, good Sheriff, you should have cut out his tongue first. You should keep silent and secret if you expect this bogey Robin Hood to come to his aid, as I've heard tell he does. Why, this man's cries will waken the King in Palestine, or wherever he is now!'

'Silence, you dog!' cried the Sheriff, striking the serf roughly across the mouth. 'You ought to know better than to make this unseemly noise in the presence of His Royal Highness Prince John!'

'Prince John! Prince John!' gasped the man. 'Oh, save me, sire! For God's love, save me!'

'Who is he?' asked John casually. 'What has he done?'

'They call him Much,' said the Sheriff importantly. 'He was a miller once. But he was too fond of the King's deer. See, his first and second fingers have been cut off: that tells its own story – a bowstring pulled unlawfully. Now we've caught him at it again: the law lays it down that for a second conviction for deer-slaying, a man shall have his eyes burnt out. A third time – and he hangs. But I'll warrant he'll find it hard to shoot a deer when we've done with him: I've never known a man to shoot by smell – ha! ha!'

The Sheriff laughed heartily at his own joke, and Prince John was pleased to smile.

'Well, fellow?' he said to poor old Much, who still knelt trembling before him.

'So please your highness,' gasped Much, 'they burnt my mill to make a wider hunting-ground and a way to the stream so that the deer could come there to drink. How could I get my food but by hunting? It's hard to shoot straight and true lacking the arrow fingers, and true and straight must a man shoot if he would kill lawful game, the rabbit and the wood-pigeon . . . I had two children, one died of want, and my boy, young Much, was crying out for food . . . We cannot live long upon grass and herbs like an ox, nor upon the roots that the swine eat.'

'Oh,' said Prince John, 'so you decided to try a richer diet, did you? The king's deer! . . . Was there no other way? No, no, Master Sheriff, let me deal justly with him . . . What of this Robin Hood of whom tales are told? Some rich man, they say – a yeoman or a nobleman born of some old Saxon family – who, mad fool, brings help to such dirt as you and your kin of law breakers,

'These rogues are too loyal for my liking'

kills the king's deer himself, and has even robbed a purse on the highway before now. . . . Well, where is he? And, more to the point, *who* is he? Tell me that, and you shall keep your eyes – to see your way to the gallows one day, I'll be bound!'

'I know not who he is!' gasped Much. 'Robin Hood comes out of the forest – men say he is the Good Spirit of Sherwood – and having brought help, he goes away as silently as he came. No one has seen him by daylight . . .'

'Faugh!' cried Prince John impatiently. 'Take him away and do your work on him out of my sight. These rogues are too loyal for my liking, or for their own good.'

So four of the Sheriff's men dragged poor Much away while a fifth drew the glowing irons from the fire which had been his home and followed grimly at his heels. But suddenly with a desperate cry he tore himself loose, snatched a sword from one of them, and made a rush at Prince John. He never reached him, however, for with a sudden vicious whine an arrow sped from behind them and laid him dead on the ground.

'A good shot, truly,' remarked Prince John, 'though I could wish that it had but maimed him. A dead man is no bait for this Robin Hood . . . Who was it loosed this arrow?'

He turned as he spoke, and saw advancing towards him from the edge of the glade a short dark man wearing a green cloak over his suit of brown leather.

'My lord,' said the man, bowing very low before Prince John, 'I am called Worman, Steward to Robert Fitzooth, Earl of Huntingdon.'

Prince John's smile twisted itself suddenly into a scowl of anger.

'Earl of Huntingdon, indeed!' he exclaimed, 'I have heard tell of this nonsense before – David Lord Carrick is the Earl – Northumberland's son. What pretence is this?'

'Pardon me, my lord,' protested Worman, cringing before Prince John. 'Hereabouts men call Fitzooth Earl of Huntingdon, by right of his mother and the Saxon line of the old Earls. He is my master, so I dare not call him otherwise!'

Prince John nodded. 'I would know more of this supposed Earl,' he said in his most cruel and silky tones. 'Is he loyal, think you?'

'To King Richard – yes,' answered Worman with meaning in his voice.

'Richard – Richard – everywhere Richard!' snarled John. 'Richard is dead – or as good as dead – rotting in some dungeon. That mad minstrel Blondel will never find him! I am King: King in all but name ... This fellow Fitzooth: is he rich? Are his lands wide?'

'Once they were wide indeed,' said Worman, 'but now only the house and lands of Locksley remain to him. The other lands he has sold.'

'Ha, then his coffers must be full of gold!' cried Prince John.

'Even I his Steward do not know that,' answered Worman. 'I know only that he has some secret need for money, though what it is he keeps to himself and no one in his household knows except his friend and body-servant William Scathlock.'

'How could I see him unknown?' mused Prince John. 'If I heard but a word of treason – well, we would see what was in those coffers. . . . And you, my good fellow, should have your pickings – if you prove true and secret.'

'Against my master?' said Worman. 'Can I betray him? . . . But indeed my duty to you, sire, overweighs all other duties. . . . Then I will tell you how it can be done. Tomorrow Earl Robert is to be married at Fountains Abbey to the Lady Marian, daughter of Lord Fitzwalter. Tonight he holds a great feast in his own great house of Locksley Hall: all guests will be welcome and no close watch kept as to who they are. If you and

the Sheriff come disguised – as palmers from the Holy
Land, perhaps, with some tall tale of King Richard –
you will have a ready welcome.'

'I like the scheme,' exclaimed Prince John who, for
all his faults, never lacked courage. 'Come with me,
good fellow; and you, Master Sheriff, gather your men
and come also: we have little time to waste. Leave that
dead dog there – as a warning to Robin Hood should he
come this way.'

When they had ridden off into the grey of the evening,
and silence had fallen upon Sherwood once again, certain bent and maimed figures began to creep out of the
nearby thickets and gather round the body of old Much
the miller which lay where it had fallen near the still
smoking ashes of his home.

'He's dead,' exclaimed one of them. 'Well, better
than blinding. . . . These are cruel times.'

'Aye,' cried another, 'but when the King comes home
from the Crusade, things will be better.'

'But if he never comes back,' muttered a third, 'then
that devil Prince John will be King – and God have
mercy on us then.'

'Here's that poor lad Much, son of the man they've
murdered,' interrupted another. 'What can we do for
him? The old man went out to shoot a deer, for hunger
drove him to it. . . . Which of us can feed this poor
orphan lad?'

There was a general murmur of pity while the boy
Much knelt weeping by his father's body. Then some-
body said quietly:

'Robin Hood will not let him starve. Look, here
comes his man, Will Scarlet, carrying a sack. May God
and Our Lady bless this Robin Hood who comes to our
aid like some very angel.'

A man had walked quickly into their midst as he spoke, a tall man of some forty years of age whose costume of russet and scarlet well suited the name by which these poor outcasts knew him.

'Have courage, my friends!' cried Will Scarlet, lowering the heavy sack as he spoke. 'My master and your true friend Robin Hood has sent me with this, fearing lest you should hunger. For he knows that the Sheriff and his men have been out in the Forest this day – and they ever leave misery and want behind them.'

'God's blessing on brave Robin Hood!' chorused all of them, except the boy who still knelt weeping by the still body.

Scarlet went over to him and laid a hand gently on his shoulder.

'So they have killed old Much,' he said. 'Have comfort, boy: he is at peace, and has been spared many evils. It was a quick death, see the arrow has transfixed his heart. . . . Strange, that arrow never came from Nottingham armoury: it is such a one as my master and his servants use.'

'Good Will Scarlet!' cried the boy, turning to him suddenly. 'Let me come with you and serve your noble master too. I know I am but twelve years old – but sorrow brings us quickly to manhood – and I would be revenged on these accursed murderers.'

'Speak not of revenge,' said Will Scarlet gently. 'It is for justice that we fight . . . But come with me. We have need of a bold lad like you – and one who can be trusted, even to the death as your father could be trusted.'

'Aye, aye,' chorused the group round about them. 'Be sure the old man died rather than betray your master, and so would any one of us. God save Robin Hood – King Richard and Robin Hood!'

CHAPTER TWO

HOW ROBERT OF LOCKSLEY BECAME AN OUTLAW

This youth that leads yon virgin by the hand
Is our Earl Robert, or your Robin Hood
That in these days was Earl of Huntingdon;
The ill-fac'd miser, brib'd in either hand,
Is Worman, once the steward of his house,
Who, Judas like, betrays his liberal lord.

ANTHONY MUNDAY: *The Downfall of Robert*
Earl of Huntingdon (1601)

IN Locksley Hall that night all seemed peaceful and happy enough as his friends and tenants feasted in honour of Robert Fitzooth's wedding with Marian Fitzwalter which was to take place on the morrow.

Earl Robert stood near the great fireplace welcoming his guests: a fine, well-built man of some thirty years, handsome, brown-haired with a short beard and clear eyes behind which seemed to lurk a shadow – of pity and of determination. All his movements were quick, but none of them was hurried; he was the man of action, the leader who could see things clearly and, in a flash, deliver his order and act upon his decision with swift accuracy and perfect coolness.

The Lady Marian Fitzwalter stood beside him. She was some five years younger than he, tall and beautiful, but strong and fearless also, a very fitting wife for such a man.

So certainly thought most of those present, as they came up in turns to offer their congratulations, or their services according to rank, or joined from time to time in a hearty song followed by the old Saxon pledge of 'Waes hēal!' as they raised their goblets or silver-mounted horns of mead or ale to the two of them.

Two palmers however, who had come in late, led by Worman the steward, did not seem so eager in their toasts.

'I smell treason, there's no doubt of it!' muttered the darker of the two.

'It's a whole nest of traitors, your Highness,' agreed his companion. 'They'll give us proof before long, you may depend upon it!'

As if to bear out his words, a group of foresters dressed all in Lincoln green, who stood near the door, began to sing:

> Long live Richard,
> Robin and Richard!
> Long live Richard!
> Down with John!
> Drink to the Lion-heart
> Everyone!

'Down with John, indeed!' said the dark palmer grimly. 'Now I trust that my disguise is good – and that master Worman, the false steward, won't waver again in his loyalties! Hallo, what have we here?'

As the song ended there was a slight stir near the doorway and a tall forester dressed in russet and scarlet appeared pushing his way through the throng, and leading a boy by the hand.

The second palmer stiffened suddenly like a pointer-dog smelling game.

'My lord,' he whispered to his companion. 'That boy is the son of old Much the miller whom you saw shot this afternoon when he escaped from those who would so justly have burned out his eyes for deer-slaying on a second charge.'

'Indeed, my good Sheriff,' replied the supposed palmer. 'This false Earl Robert harbours the sons of traitors and criminals, does he? ... But here comes Master Worman.'

'How now, Master Worman?' asked the disguised Sheriff in an undertone. 'What does this mean?'

'Yonder is Earl Robert's man, William Scathlock,' answered Worman, 'and he brings with him the son of that traitor who threatened your highness this afternoon, and in whose black heart I was lucky enough to plant an arrow.'

'Well?'

'Your Highness, when I inquired for Much the Miller's son – never mind from whom – they told me that all was well with him since a certain Will Scarlet had come and taken him away to be cared for by Robin Hood!'

'Will Scarlet! ... Robin Hood,' mused Prince John. 'The devil! ... Master Worman, and you, good Sir Sheriff, we are in better luck than ever we dreamed of! Do you not see? Will Scarlet takes Much to the care of Robin Hood ... William Scathlock brings that same Much to the care of Robert Fitzooth – to that false Earl Robert who sells his lands and uses the proceeds so mysteriously ... Why, my good fellows, it is proof positive ... And that song they were singing:

> Long live Richard,
> Robin and Richard!

Yes, there's no doubt of it. ... Well, your fortunes are made. Tomorrow this traitor Robert or Robin is declared an outlaw – and you take and hang him forthwith. Then of course all his lands and goods are forfeit to me: I take them – and that attractive young heiress the Lady Marian lacks a husband . . . She has one waiting for her though, as I know well, and one true to my cause . . . Yes, Sir Guy of Gisborne shall have her – and with her father's good will, or I am much mistaken in my man . . . And Sir Guy shall pay me a fine fat dowry for his bride!'

No one suspected the two supposed palmers at Earl Robert's feast, but none the less there was an air of anxiety over the wedding preparations in the chapel of Fountains Abbey next day.

Lord Fitzwalter seemed troubled and uneasy, though his daughter Marian was calm enough, even though she and her father stood waiting at the altar some time before Earl Robert rode up to the door with his troop of bowmen. Placing his men in the aisles in military formation – much to Lord Fitzwalter's surprise and the Abbot's indignation – Earl Robert only then came forward to take his place beside Marian.

Looking anything but pleased, the fat little Abbot began to intone the ceremony, his long lines of monks chanting the responses in the wide chancel behind him.

But before ever the words were spoken which would make Robert and Marian man and wife, there came the sound of galloping hooves, the clash and jingle of armour, and into the chapel strode a knight with a drawn sword in his hand and followed by a band of men at arms.

'What means this sacrilege?' cried the Abbot, torn between fear and indignation.

'Hold!' cried the knight. 'I, Sir Guy of Gisborne, come in the King's name to forbid this ceremony to proceed! Pursuivant, read the mandate!'

A man dressed in the livery of the Sheriff of Nottingham stepped forward, unrolled a parchment, and read in a loud voice:

'Be it known to all, in the name of Prince John, Regent of all England, that Robert Fitzooth, known as Robert Earl of Huntingdon – known also as Robin Hood; for as much as he hath aided the King's enemies, broken the King's laws, and is a traitor to the King and to those by him set in authority; that the same Robert Fitzooth or Robin Hood is hereby declared outlaw, his lands and goods forfeit, and his person proscribed and banished. In the name of Richard our King and of the Regent, Prince John!'

'Sir Guy,' said Robert quietly, 'this is an ill quest you come on, and all unworthy of the high order of knighthood which you profess. As for this mandate, I question its force! Show me King Richard's seal attached to it. ... You cannot. Show me then the seal of My Lord Bishop of Ely the King's only lawfully appointed Regent. ... Why, that is missing from the mandate also! ... Tell me wherein I have played the part of a traitor – and wherefore I, Robert Fitzooth, Esquire of Locksley and Earl of Huntingdon, should answer for the supposed misdeeds of this mythical wood-demon called Robin Hood who is surely no more than a bogey raised by the credulity and superstition of the ignorant!'

Guy of Gisborne laughed harshly.

'This is no time for jests and fairy tales,' he cried. 'We all know that you have ever flouted the laws and striven to set the serfs against their masters. Why, the very act of calling yourself Earl of Huntingdon in right of your mother's Saxon forbears shows you as a traitor: the old Saxon earls were deprived and outlawed for refusing to obey their rightful King, William of Normandy, and only the Earldom created by the King has any right in law. As for your trespasses in the matter of the Forest Laws – everyone knows your skill in archery – and there are few travellers in these parts who have not eaten the King's venison under your roof. Finally, it is useless to pretend ignorance of the crimes committed by you under the false name of Robin Hood. How many among your own followers are proscribed felons who are said to belong to Robin Hood's band? ... What of his lieutenant who is also of your household? ... What of Much, the Miller's son, whom Robin Hood has under his care – in *your* house of Locksley Hall?'

'Why then,' came the quiet answer, 'here and now Robert Fitzooth, Earl of Huntingdon, ceases to be. You have called me Robin Hood: both you and your Sheriff – yes and Prince John himself shall live to fear that name. And not only you, but all those like you: the abbots and bishops who grow fat on the sufferings of the poor; the Norman knights and barons who break both the King's law and the law of God in their cruelties and oppressions – yes, and all their kind shall go in terror so long as Robin Hood reigns in Sherwood Forest: in Sherwood, and wherever else wrongs need to be righted – until King Richard comes home from the Crusade and there is justice once more in this fair land of England.'

Then, turning to Marian Fitzwalter who had stood all this while by his side, Robin said gently:

'Lady Marian, did you give your love to the Earl of Huntingdon whose lands stretch from the Trent to the Ouse, or to plain Robin Hood the outlaw who returns now to the home of his birth under the green leaves of Sherwood Forest?'

'Neither to the Earl nor to his Earldom,' answered Marian firmly, 'but to the man whom I love and whose wife alone I shall be.'

'Indeed, I thought no other,' said Robin gravely,

'and though the ceremony is but half completed, I hold that we are none the less man and wife in the sight of God and of this congregation ... Lord Fitzwalter, to your care I commit your daughter: guard her well at Arlingford Castle, and I will demand her of you again when King Richard is here to place her hand in mine.'

'To that also I swear!' cried Marian. 'You, Robin, are my lord and my husband, and no other shall ever be aught to me, though I live and die a maid!'

'Go quickly now,' said Robin to Lord Fitzwalter, 'and go you quickly with him, sweet Marian. No, you cannot help me: when I have beaten off these curs, I ride to the merry greenwood, there to set up my court!'

'Come now, false traitor and outlaw Robin Hood!' cried Guy of Gisborne. 'Out of your own mouth are you convicted of treason many times over before this company – whom I call upon to witness ... Come now, deliver up your sword and submit yourself to the authority of your undoubted lord, Prince John. If you do so, there may still be mercy for you!'

'He knows of no mercy!' cried Robin. 'Prince John knows only the desires of his own evil heart – and you do ill to serve him ... As for my sword, I deliver it up to John and his officers – thus!'

With a sudden lightning movement Robin whipped the sword from his side and smote Guy of Gisborne such a blow upon his iron helmet that he stumbled and fell to the ground insensible. Then he charged down the nave, his men closing in from either side as he went, and a short sharp battle took place near the chapel door.

'Help! Murder! Sacrilege!' shouted the fat Abbot, and his monks and friars took up the cry as they pushed and crowded in their eagerness to escape through the narrow door which led to the Abbey. They were speeded on their way by an occasional arrow from Robin's

'As for my sword, I deliver it – thus!'

archers who continued to send shaft after shaft among
Sir Guy's followers until they too fell back towards the
door by which the Abbot had already squeezed his way
into safety.

When the sound of horses' hooves told him that Lord
Fitzwalter with Marian and their followers were well
away in the direction of Arlingford Castle, Robin gave
the signal to his men, and with one determined charge
they were out of the chapel and away through Sherwood
Forest in the direction of Locksley Hall.

Sir Guy, still half stunned, was only just raising himself from the floor of the chapel, and Robin had disappeared with all his following into the green depths of
Sherwood by the time he had gathered his wits and
staggered to his feet.

'There's no use in following him now, God's malaison
upon this rogue Fitzooth and his friends!' he exclaimed.
'But he'll find the Sheriff and Master Worman waiting
for him at Locksley Hall if he ventures there!'

Bidding those of his followers who still stood upon
their feet attend to those whom Robin's followers had
laid out on the chapel floor, Sir Guy made his way into
the Abbey, where the Abbot was only too ready to
entertain him to dinner.

'An unholy scoundrel!' spluttered the Abbot, who
needed his goblet filling again and yet again with choice
wine before he could recover from the shock to his dig-
nity and the terror of those terrible whizzing arrows.
'He is well outlawed. May a blessing rest upon the head
of the man who cuts him off!'

'A dangerous fellow,' agreed Sir Guy, putting his
hand to his aching head. 'And I grieve that he escaped
us for now he will grow more dangerous.'

'Earl Robert is a worthy man,' remarked a friar who
was quite the tallest, broadest, and reddest in the face of

any there. 'He is the best marksman in England and can outshoot any forester or archer both for distance and for directness of aim.'

'Brother Michael! Brother Michael!' puffed the Abbot. 'You speak treason! How can an outlaw be a worthy man? And as for his skill as an archer – '

'He will draw the long bow with any yeoman,' interrupted Brother Michael placidly, 'and split a willow wand at two hundred paces!'

'Be that as it may,' said Sir Guy, glowering at the friar, 'he is an outlaw now – and the sooner an arrow reaches his heart the better.'

'It is a dangerous thing to outlaw such a man,' boomed Brother Michael. 'You have taken his home: where will he live? Why, in the Forest! You have taken his cattle and his swine: what will he eat? Why, the King's deer! You have robbed him of money and goods – why then, he will rob you and all of your kind. Oh-ho, no knight nor sheriff, no abbot nor bishop will be safe from him now!'

'All the more reason why we should catch him swiftly and string him to a gallows!' snapped Sir Guy. 'But father Abbot, tell me of the Lady Marian: how came Lord Fitzwalter to betroth her to such a man as Fitzooth – for surely neither father nor daughter can have been ignorant that he was Robin Hood?'

'Oh, she is a fine lass, truly!' cried Brother Michael before the Abbot could get in a word. 'I am her confessor, and indeed I should know! Has she not beauty, grace, wit, good sense and high valour? Can she not fence with the sword, ply the quarter-staff and shoot with the long bow all but as well as – as Robin Hood himself? Truly a worthy mate for a worthy man: I would, sir knight, that you had delayed your coming but a brief half-hour, and a knot would have been tied that all our usurper Prince John's mandates could not have untied.'

'My sword would have cut it soon enough!' shouted Sir Guy. 'And it is only your cloth, master friar, that saves your head from feeling the edge of that same sword.'

'Oh, the penances I will impose upon you for this!' began the Abbot, turning to Brother Michael and almost bursting with rage.

'Why then, holy father,' cried the friar, 'I will not be here to suffer them! I have a ready welcome at Arlingford Castle – and thither I will hasten and take up my abode.'

'And I will accompany you,' said Guy of Gisborne grimly. 'This paragon of beauty, the Lady Marian, is well worth a visit – and may well prove a bait that will draw this outlawed Robin Hood into a trap!'

CHAPTER THREE

THE OUTLAWS OF SHERWOOD FOREST

An hundred valiant men had this brave Robin Hood,
Still ready at his call, that bowmen were right good,
All clad in Lincoln green, with caps of red and blue,
His fellow's winded horn not one of them but knew . . .
All made of Spanish yew, their bows were wondrous strong;
They not an arrow drew but was a clothyard long.

MICHAEL DRAYTON: *Polyolbion* xxvi (1622)

EARLY next morning Sir Guy of Gisborne set out for Arlingford Castle, his guide being the fat friar called Brother Michael who had so disgraced himself on the previous night by praising the outlawed Robin Hood.

The friar rode at his side singing lustily – in spite of the fact that as they left the Abbey, the Abbot had banished him in no uncertain terms: 'You go out, false and traitorous man, as you came in many years ago: – plain Michael Tuck – no longer a Brother of this Order. If you show your face at my doors again, my doors will be shut in your face!'

'Why then!' cried the Friar gaily, 'farewell to the Abbey of Fountains, and all hail to the jolly greenwood – and catch me again if you can!'

So he went on his way, singing:

For hark! hark! hark!
The dog doth bark,
*   That watches the wild deer's lair,*
The hunter awakes at the peep of the dawn,
But the lair it is empty, the deer it is gone,
*   And the hunter knows not where!*

As they came in sight of Arlingford Castle the Friar ceased from his singing, and turning to Sir Guy, remarked:

'You had best turn back, sir knight – or at the least lower that vizor of yours!'

'How?' exclaimed Guy of Gisborne. 'Surely Lord Fitzwalter is not in league with Robin Hood?'

'Far from it!' laughed the fat Friar, 'but Lady Marian Fitzwalter assuredly is. And Lady Marian is as apt with an arrow as most damsels are with a needle!'

They reached the castle in safety, however, and Lord Fitzwalter welcomed them loudly, showing great eagerness to be on the side in power:

'You have done me a wrong? How so? Would you have had me marry my daughter to an outlaw, a fly-by-night, a slayer of the King's deer – and of the Prince's followers? A man who flings away an earldom, broad lands and rich treasures to help a lot of miserable serfs and other riff-raff most justly persecuted by the laws of the land. No, sir, no: you have done me a service. A great service. I have finished with Fitzooth, or Robin Hood, or whatever that rascally beggar now calls himself. And so has my daughter.'

'And yet she is half wedded to him by the dictates of the church,' remarked the Friar, 'and wholly his by the dictates of her heart.'

'The marriage was not completed!' shouted Lord Fitzwalter. 'Therefore I care nothing for it. As for love – it is your business, as her confessor, to show her that her love for this traitor is sinful and to be stamped out!'

'Marriages,' quoth the Friar, 'are made in Heaven. Love is God's work – and it is not for me to meddle with it.'

'The ceremony was cut short – sure proof that Heaven laid no blessing on it!' roared Lord Fitzwalter. 'Besides,

I betrothed my daughter to the Earl of Huntingdon, not to the outlawed traitor Robin Hood.'

'He may be pardoned,' answered the Friar. 'Cœur de Lion is a worthy king – and Fitzooth a worthy peer.'

'There can be no pardon,' said Sir Guy hastily. 'He has killed the king's subjects and defied the king's sheriff.'

Lord Fitzwalter was growing more and more red in the face with fury, but at this moment the Lady Marian came suddenly into the room, clad in Lincoln green, with a quiver of arrows at her side and a bow in her hand.

'How now?' roared her father. 'Where are you off to now, wench?'

'To the greenwood,' said Marian calmly.

'That you shall not!' bellowed Lord Fitzwalter.

'But I am going,' said Marian.

'But I will have up the drawbridge.'

'But I will swim the moat.'

'But I will secure the gates.'

'But I will leap from the battlement.'

'But I will lock you in an upper chamber.'

'But I will shred the tapestry and let myself down.'

'But I will lock you in a turret where you shall only see light through a loophole.'

'But I will find some way of escape. And, father, while I go freely, I shall return willingly. But once shut me up, and if I slip out then, I shall not return at all . . . Robin waits for me in the greenwood, and the knot half-tied yesterday can so easily be tied completely.'

'Well spoken, lady,' cried the Friar.

'Ill spoken, Friar!' thundered Lord Fitzwalter. 'Get out of my castle this instant! You are in league with the traitor Robin Hood, I know it! If you come here again, I'll have you whipped, monk or no monk!'

'I go, I go!' said the Friar calmly. 'I know of a hermitage by the riverside where I may well take up my abode — and levy toll on all those who would pass by: payment, of course, for my prayers! Abbey and castle have cast me out, but not so easily shall Friar Tuck be cast down!'

And away he strode, singing blithely:

> *For I must seek some hermit cell,*
> *Where I alone my beads may tell,*
> *And on the wight who that way fares*
> *Levy a toll for my ghostly pray'rs!*

'So much for an impudent friar!' puffed Lord Fitzwalter. 'Now for a wayward girl!'

'A husband,' said Sir Guy with meaning, 'is the best curb for such as she.'

'Aye, a husband — and of my choosing!' agreed Lord Fitzwalter. 'No more earls of doubtful earldoms, but, shall we say, a knight with definite lands and treasures, and definitely in favour with Prince John! Such a man, in fact, as — well, no matter!'

Lord Fitzwalter looked Guy of Gisborne up and down with approval, but Marian broke out:

'No man of your choosing, father — unless he be my choice also. And my choice is and will ever be for brave Robin Hood!'

'I'll keep you in a dungeon and feed you on bread and water!' thundered Lord Fitzwalter.

'Robin will sack your castle to rescue me,' said Marian gaily. Then suddenly serious, she exclaimed: 'Father, you will let me go to the greenwood? You have my promise that I will return. And I promise also that Robin shall be nothing more to me than he is now, without your leave — or until King Richard return and give me to him in marriage with his own hand.'

Then, blowing a kiss to her father, and paying no attention whatsoever to Guy of Gisborne, Marian tripped gaily from the room and away into Sherwood Forest.

'And now,' said Lord Fitzwalter grimly, 'it is for you to catch this outlaw and string him up to the highest gallows in Nottinghamshire. Until that is done, I fear there will be no use in your coming here to ask my daughter's hand in marriage.'

Sir Guy rose and bowed to his host.

'My lord,' he said, 'I am already on my way to Locksley Hall. The Sheriff's men were to surround it last night, taking prisoner any who came in or out, and my followers do but await me at the Abbey. When I get there, it may well be to find Robin Hood already in their hands.'

But Robert Fitzooth had not been so unaware of the dangers into which his double life as Robin Hood was leading him as the Sheriff and Prince John had supposed. When he escaped from the chapel after the interrupted wedding, Robin and some twenty men at arms rode off into Sherwood Forest and continued on their way to within a mile or so of Locksley Hall. Here Robin halted and turning, spoke to his followers:

'My friends, what I feared has befallen me. You all heard the mandate of outlawry read against me – and some of you may have incurred danger of the same by withstanding those men sent against me under Sir Guy of Gisborne. Well now, you may choose for yourselves: I set you all free from my service – but indeed as I am an outlaw, that sets you free whether I will or no. If you did not all know it already, you know now that I am that Robin Hood who, for several years now, has befriended all such as suffer under the cruelty and unjustness of lords, barons, bishops, abbots, and sheriffs. I have

already a band of men sworn to follow me who await
me in the greenwood: we are all comrades and brothers,
though me they have chosen to be their leader and their
king – not because I am by right an Earl, not merely
because I have the gift of a steady hand and a clear eye
and so can shoot an arrow further and straighter than
most men, but because one must rule and I come of a
race of rulers (though we are but slaves now to our
Norman masters). I am no more Robert Fitzooth, Earl
of Huntingdon, but the plain yeoman of Locksley whom
men call Robin Hood: but my friends in Sherwood have
chosen me king, and a king in Sherwood I shall be, my
first care for my followers, but our first care for justice
and mercy and the Love of God. And in this I hold that
we commit no treason: when Richard comes home from
the Crusade this reign of terror and of evil against which
I fight will end. Cruel, lawless John will oppress us no
longer, nor his friends and followers use us without right
or justice, as slaves and not as free men.

'Choose now, will you follow me into Sherwood, all
such of you as have neither wife nor child – or, as you
blamelessly may, go back to serve the new master of
Locksley. Only, for the love and service that was between us, I charge you to betray neither me nor any
who were your companions and are now mine.'

Then most of the men at arms cried aloud that they
would follow Robin Hood through weal and woe, and
all swore that they would die rather than betray him.
Some then turned and with bent heads rode off towards
Locksley – drawn thither by wife or child – and swore
reluctantly to serve Sir Guy of Gisborne so long as he
might be the master of Locksley.

'And now,' said Robin to those who remained with
him, 'let us away to our new home in the forest and see
how many of us there be who stand loyally together for

God, for His anointed servant Richard, King by right divine, and for justice and the righting of wrongs.'

Deep in the heart of Sherwood Forest, as the sun was setting behind them, Robin and his men came to a great glade where stood the greatest of all the forest oaks upon a stretch of open greensward with steep banks fencing it on either hand in which were caves both deep and dry. At either end of the shallow valley, and beyond the banks on each side, the forest hedged them in with its mighty trees, with oak and ash, with beech and elm and chestnut, and also with thick clumps of impassable thorns, with desolate marshes where an unwary step might catch a man or a horse and drag him down into the dark quagmire, and with brambles rising like high dykes and knolls through which even a man in armour could scarcely force his way.

For the last mile Robin led by narrow, winding paths, pointing out to his companions the secret, hidden signs by which they could find their way.

Once in the glade, Robin took the horn from his belt and blew on it a blast which echoed away and away into the distance. Already men dressed smartly in doublet and hose of Lincoln green, in hoods of green or russet and in knee-boots of soft brown leather, had come out from the caves to greet them.

At a few brief words, they set about lighting two great fires near the oak tree in the glade, and roasting great joints of venison before them. They also brought coarse loaves of brown bread, and rolled out two barrels of ale, setting up rough trestle tables with logs in lieu of stools.

As the darkness grew, men kept appearing silently in the glade and taking their place by the fires or at the tables until a company of fifty or sixty was gathered together.

'Outlaws, but not robbers'

Then Robin Hood rose up and addressed them. He began by telling them, as he had told the men at arms, of his banishment, and reminding them that they were outlaws, but not robbers.

'We must take the King's deer,' he ended, 'since we must eat to live. But when the King returns I myself will beg pardon at his feet for this trespass. And now you shall all swear the oath which I swear with you, and all seeking to join us must swear also. We declare war upon all of those thieves, robbers, extortioners and men of evil whom we find among the nobles, the clergy, and burgesses of town – in particular those who follow or accompany Prince John; false abbots, monks, bishops and archbishops, whom we will beat and bind like sheaves of corn so that they may yield the golden grain of their robberies – the Abbots of St Mary's, Doncaster, and Fountains shall we seek for in particular; and I think we shall keep within our oath if we make it our especial care to harry and persecute the false Sheriff of Nottingham who so wickedly abuses his power to please and satisfy his master Prince John.

'Now, my friends, we do not take from these and their kind to enrich ourselves. We take for the general good, and it shall be as much our duty to seek out the poor, the needy, the widow, the orphan and all those who have suffered or are suffering wrong, and minister to their wants in so far as we can.

'We shall swear, moreover, to harm no woman, be she Norman or Saxon, high or low, but to succour and assist any who crave our aid or need our protection, dealing with them with all honesty and purity, seeing in every woman the likeness of Our Lady the Holy Mary, Mother of Christ, in whose name we take our oath, and by whose name we dedicate ourselves to the service of the true Church, and to whom we pray to intercede for

us before the throne of God that we may have strength
to keep this our oath in the face of all temptations.'

Then, in that wild and lonely glade, while the owls
screamed over the dark forest, and an occasional wolf
howled in the distance, they all knelt down together and
swore their oath – a pledge as high and as sacred, though
they were but outlaws and escaped felons, as that sworn
by the noblest knight who, in the days when the Saxons
themselves were the conquerors and oppressors, had sat
at King Arthur's Table.

CHAPTER FOUR

THE RESCUE OF WILL SCARLET

And these will strike for England
And man and maid be free
To foil and spoil the tyrant
Beneath the greenwood tree.

TENNYSON: *The Foresters (1881)*

EARLY the next morning after he had gathered his band in Sherwood Forest and sworn his great oath with them, Robin Hood sent Will Scarlet and Much, the Miller's son, to see what had happened at Locksley Hall.

Walking briskly through the forest, by many winding paths, all of which were known to Scarlet, they came to the edge of the open parkland in the middle of which stood the grey stone house with its square tower at one corner made for defence.

The morning sun glittered now on the armour and weapons of the Sheriff's men who stood guard both on the tower top and at the great door of the hall itself, while outside stood a crowd of poorer people amongst whom Scarlet recognized most of those who had been tenants or serfs under the Fitzooth family, or personal servants at the Hall.

'Now,' said Scarlet, when they had watched for some time, 'I think that, without undue danger, I might mingle with those who were my fellows, and perhaps even do my late master a good service. But do you wait here – for you are in danger if any of the Sheriff's men see you.'

So saying, Will Scarlet laid down his bow and arrows

beside Much, tightened his belt, drew his hood forward so as to shadow his face, and walked quietly out from among the trees.

He was greeted in subdued voices by one or two of the yeomen who stood around the door, and soon learnt from them that the Sheriff and his men were inside, taking possession of the place in the name of Prince John and deciding which of Robin's tenants were still to hold their lands.

'Those who can pay out a good round sum as a present to Prince John,' an old yeoman informed Scarlet, 'may well become tenants to our new master – and better still if they can give the Sheriff a gift also – not forgetting Steward Worman who has his ear in these matters.'

'Well,' said Scarlet, 'I have no desire to serve any but our true liege lord King Richard – and under him, Fitzooth of Locksley, or none! But now I bethink me, I have the hard savings of twenty years' service: surely these new masters would not rob us of our savings?'

'All but a tithe we may take away, good Scathlock,' an old man who had been William Fitzooth's groom told him. 'That tenth part they take as a fine for our faithful service to our true masters: may all the saints bless good Earl Robert, and bring him back to his rightful inheritance!'

'Amen!' said Will Scarlet, and strode quietly into the house, along the side of the great hall, and so away to the little garret room which had been his. Taking from his pouch a large key, he unlocked a wooden chest which stood there, and from beneath a pile of clothes drew out two leather bags – one large and the other small. The large one he packed carefully with some of the clothes into a bundle; the small one he placed in the pouch from which he had taken the key.

Then he walked quietly down the little stone stair in the Hall, and strove to slip away as unnoticed as he had come. He might have succeeded in this, for no one appeared to be keeping watch at the door, if he had not had the misfortune to come out into the sunshine just as Sir Guy of Gisborne and his small band of armed men arrived from Fountains Abbey.

'Ah-ha!' said Sir Guy. 'What have we here?'

'So please you, my lord,' answered Scarlet humbly, 'I was a servant here for twenty years, and now that my late master is outlawed, I go forth to seek my fortune elsewhere.'

'Well, if you will not stay to serve me, the new master of Locksley,' said Sir Guy, 'I will certainly not strive to keep you against your will. But what have you there?'

'No more than my humble possessions,' replied Scarlet. 'This bundle of clothes, with iron cap and hood of chain mail; and here in my pouch ten gold nobles, all that I have saved these many years against my old age.'

'Oh, pass, pass!' cried Sir Guy impatiently. 'Our quarrel is with Robin Hood the outlaw, not with those who served him as Robert Fitzooth – though I dare say most of them knew of his treason.'

'Thank you, my lord,' said Scarlet, and slinging the bundle over his shoulder, he strode away towards the bushes behind which Much was hiding.

But at that moment, hearing the sounds made by Guy and his followers, Worman the false steward came out of the house, and saw Scarlet making off with the bundle over his back.

'Stop that man!' he cried. 'We have not searched his possessions – nor has he paid his tithe by way of fine.'

'You do the fellow wrong,' said Sir Guy haughtily. 'The goods are his: only those of Earl Robert are forfeit.'

'Of the traitor Robin Hood!' shouted Worman excitedly. 'Yes! Well, how know we that this fellow is not making off with some of his master's possessions? There should be a bag of gold, got from the sale of land, and jewels worth much gold, neither of which have we found.'

'That alters the case, certainly,' said Sir Guy, and turning round, he bade two of his mounted followers ride after Scarlet and bring him back.

Scarlet was near the bushes by this time – but he had heard what was happening, since Worman had been shouting in his anger and eagerness. Springing into cover, he flung down the bundle, tore it open and snatched out the bag of money and jewels.

'Much!' he hissed. 'Guard that with your life, and take it to Robin Hood. Say that to save it from his enemies was my last service. Quick! There is no escape for me: Worman will recognize me at once. Do not answer, run – hide!'

While he spoke, Scarlet was fastening the bundle again. Now he glanced back through the bushes:

'No time to run!' he muttered to Much. 'Here! Into that hollow tree! Now, silence whatever happens!'

Much scrambled hastily up an elm-stump and tumbled with his bag of treasure into the hollow trunk – where he found himself in a nest of young owls.

He was only just in time, and Scarlet had not walked more than a dozen paces deeper into the forest when the horsemen broke through the bushes, shouting:

'Stand, there! Stand!'

Scarlet turned round, and stared in surprise at the men.

'What would you with me, sirs?' he asked.

'Sir Guy would speak with you again,' he was told, and a moment later found himself led back towards the house between the two horses.

'What would you with me, my lord?' he asked humbly of Sir Guy – keeping his face hidden as much as possible from Worman as he spoke.

'Search that bundle!' commanded Sir Guy briefly. 'And the fellow's clothes.'

'No time to run! Here, into that hollow tree'

'There are but garments, and an iron head piece and a chain-mail hood,' protested Scarlet. 'And on me but the bag with my savings – my ten nobles, hardly earned these twenty years and more.'

'If you speak truth, no harm will befall you,' said Sir Guy.

'It is even as he says,' declared one of the men, spreading Scarlet's possessions out on the ground. 'Old garments, and this head-armour.'

'Yes, but what has the knave under his cloak,' began Worman, and with a sudden movement he pulled off both cloak and hood.

'Only my ten golden nobles,' began Scarlet, holding out the little bag from his pouch to Sir Guy.

But Worman had seen his face.

'It is Will Scathlock!' he cried. 'Seize him – he is a traitor! – And he can lead us to the arch-traitor his master, Robin Hood!'

Scarlet's hand flew to the long knife at his belt, but he was surrounded by Sir Guy's men, and two of them had him by the arms before ever the blade left the sheath.

'String him up from the tower top –' began Sir Guy, but Worman interposed quickly:

'Not so, my lord, let him before the Sheriff. And then away with him to Nottingham. Let him hang there to-morrow in the market square as a warning to all traitors – and in especial to all who would follow or protect Robin Hood. But before that, let us see if any persuasions will make him lead us to his master's hiding place. . . . There are dungeons at Nottingham, and in them irons that can be heated and the rack that will pull many a truth out of a stubborn man.'

'I am no traitor,' said Will Scarlet in clear, ringing tones. 'But you, Worman – you, the false Steward who grew fat upon your master's kindness, and then betrayed him – be you ware of the vengeance which just and honourable men will be waiting to bring upon you. . . . As for your irons and racks, you may spare them: Robin Hood ranges in Sherwood Forest – I can tell no more, nor would I if I could.'

After this Scarlet was led away into the Hall for some semblance of a trial before the Sheriff. Then, heavily guarded, he was taken to Nottingham and chained there in a dungeon.

Much the Miller's son missed his way several times as he threaded the narrow paths in the heart of the forest. But it was not long after noon when at last he found himself in the glade by the great tree and poured out his news to Robin Hood, after handing him the bag of gold and jewels for which Scarlet had risked so much.

When Robin heard all that had happened, he was sorely grieved.

'He must be rescued!' he cried, 'or I myself will die with him!'

'A rescue! A rescue!' shouted the outlaws who had gathered to hear Much's story. 'Let us march to Nottingham, take the place by storm and hang the Sheriff on his own gallows, with Worman beside him!'

'I would willingly hang Worman,' said Robin savagely. 'But the Sheriff does only his duty in this matter – and obeys his master Prince John. ... Also at the first hint of an attack they would withdraw into the castle, hang Will Scarlet before our eyes, and laugh to scorn our attempts at a siege. No, no – force cannot save him, but guile may. ... Come now, you, William of Goldsbrough: you served the Sheriff once, doubtless you still know all those in office – jailors, beadles, and the very hangman?'

Later that afternoon William of Goldsbrough set out alone towards Nottingham dressed in the rough leather jerkin and faded hood and hose of a man back from the wars and in search of a job.

At earliest dawn next morning Robin set out with a band picked from the youngest and strongest of his

followers, every man armed with a good broad sword
and carrying a long yew bow. All of them, however,
wore cloaks or other wraps which hid their Lincoln
green.

At the edge of the forest Robin bade them wait, sending one man forward to bring back news. Before long he
returned in company with an old man, a palmer or
pilgrim who had visited the Holy Land, muffled in
the long cloak and hood which all such wanderers
wore.

'Now tell me, good palmer,' said Robin Hood courteously, 'do you know when and where Will Scathlock
or Scarlet is to die?'

'Aye, that I do, the more's the pity,' answered the old
man. 'They brought him in last night – said he was one
of Robin Hood's men – him you know as were the Earl
of Huntingdon and helped all poor men. Well, they'll
hang Scathlock at noon on the green before the Castle:
where the May-dances should be – only today they rear
no May-pole, but a gallows.'

Rumour of the hanging had gone through Nottingham, and there was a great crowd on the green when,
punctually at noon, the Castle gates opened and out
marched the Sheriff at the head of several dozen men at
arms.

Foremost in the crowd round the gallows was an old
palmer muffled in a long cloak and hood, and leaning
on a bow in place of a staff.

'Eh!' he exclaimed in a shrill, high voice, 'Here be a
fine guard for one man! Do the Sheriff expect scuffing,
eh? A rescue, eh?'

'There's many here would swing a cudgel or ply a
quarterstaff,' said his neighbour, a yeoman farmer by
his looks, 'if Robin Hood were only here to give a lead.

Lord, we all know Will Scathlock, the Earl's man – and many a one knew him as Will Scarlet who came secretly with food and money for the poor and oppressed. Why he –'

'Hush! Hush!' hissed one or two in the crowd. 'He's speaking! Will's speaking!' The Sheriff had said something to Scarlet in a low voice, but the reply came in ringing tones:

'My name is Scathlock – and not Worman! I am no grasping villain who would betray a good and generous master for any bribe that you could offer me – no, not for my life. Robin Hood is in Sherwood Forest – you must seek him there if you would have word with him.'

'Rest assured we shall seek him!' growled the Sheriff, red with anger. 'And when we find him, burn out his eyes so that he must grope his way from Locksley to Nottingham to hang beside your rotting bones!'

There were murmurs from the crowd at this, and the Sheriff hastened on to the business in hand:

'William Scathlock or Scarlet, outlaw and traitor, the law decrees that you shall here and now be hanged by the neck, and thereafter be left hanging here as a warning to all men.'

Scarlet looked down at the crowd, and seeing no sign of rescue turned to the Sheriff. 'My lord Sheriff,' he said quietly, 'seeing that I needs must die and there is no help for it, I beg one last boon of you.'

'Speak on,' said the Sheriff. 'It is your right.'

'My noble master the Earl of Huntingdon, whom men call Robin Hood,' said Scarlet, 'had never yet one of his servants die by the dishonourable death of hanging. So now I pray you to unbind me, set a sword in my hand, and with you and all your men will I fight until you slay me.'

'Not so,' answered the Sheriff, 'this I cannot grant.'

'At least,' said Scarlet, 'unbind my hands and bid your men slay with their swords, though I myself am weaponless.'

'It cannot be,' declared the Sheriff. 'I have sworn to hang you – and even so will I hang your master, and all who follow him.'

'That will never be!' cried Scarlet. 'You dastard coward! You faint-hearted peasant slave! If ever my master shall meet with you, be sure he will pay you in full! He scorns such dastards as you, and all your coward followers: you and your paid murderers can never overcome bold Robin Hood!'

'Enough of this!' shouted the Sheriff impatiently. 'Where is the hangman? Let him do his duty without delay!'

There was a delay, nevertheless, for the hangman could not be found, and it was at last reported to the Sheriff that he lay dead-drunk in his room, having found an old friend the night before, and caroused with him until sunrise.

The Sheriff was in a great rage, particularly when he commanded first one and then another of his followers to act as hangman, and each in turn politely but firmly refused.

At last the Sheriff turned to the crowd: 'Will any one here perform this office of justice?' he demanded. 'He who undertakes it shall have a double fee.'

But the crowd only muttered and growled angrily, and the Sheriff was about to bid his men draw their swords and cut Will Scarlet down with them, since there seemed no chance of hanging him, when the old palmer suddenly stepped forward.

'Good Master Sheriff!' he cried in his shrill cracked, voice, 'I have a grudge against Will Scarlet! Let me have the task of sending him to heaven!'

'Oh, the old devil!' murmured several men in the crowd, and others showed signs of holding the palmer back.

'Come on, then,' ordered the Sheriff. 'Stand clear, everyone! Proceed, old man!'

The palmer came shuffling forward, while the crowd heaved and swayed behind him, cursing and muttering – and drawing closer and closer to the gallows.

Now Scarlet had been brought out on a low cart and left right under the gallows: all that the hangman had to do was to set the noose round his victim's neck, then get down and pull the cart away from beneath him.

Slowly and painfully the palmer scrambled on to the cart, while the curses and threats grew louder round about him, and even a clod or two of earth was hurled in his direction.

He fumbled with the rope which secured Scarlet's hands behind his back, then made as if to fit the noose over his head – whispering something to the prisoner as he did so.

Suddenly the palmer handed something from under his cloak to Will Scarlet, who dropped the rope which had bound his hands and stepped forward with a drawn sword held in front of him.

'Treachery! Help!' shouted the Sheriff. 'Down with the villain!'

But before any one could stir, Robin Hood had flung off the palmer's cloak, fitted an arrow to his bow, and shouted:

'Men of Sherwood! Freemen of England! Save this innocent man from death!'

'Robin Hood!' shouted the people.

'It is the outlawed Earl of Huntingdon!' cried the Sheriff. 'There is a great reward for anyone who takes him! Down with him!'

As he spoke the string hummed on Robin's bow, and it was the Sheriff himself who came down, amidst a yell of laughter as the arrow appeared transfixing his hat.

'The next arrow I shoot at you, Master Sheriff,' said Robin gravely, 'will be aimed two inches lower!'

'Seize him!' gasped the Sheriff, and his men sprang forward. But as they did so, the Lincoln green appeared as if by magic among the crowd, as man after man flung off their various disguises, unslung their bows or drew their swords, and ranged themselves round Robin and Scarlet.

The men at arms hesitated, and at a sign from Robin a flight of arrows sped amongst them, wounding not a few. Then they turned and fled, the Sheriff setting a good example for speed in escape.

'Now stay a while, good Master Sheriff!' jeered Scarlet. 'Let me at least thank you for my night's lodging. Stay, for now I *will* tell you where you may find Robin Hood – whom you will never catch by running in the wrong direction!'

'Let them go!' laughed Robin. 'I'll warrant we shall meet again, though. . . . Now, my friends, let us pass in peace back to the Forest. We mean no harm to any here save those who would harm us. And if any is to suffer unjustly, come one of you without fear into Sherwood and there ask for Robin Hood!'

'God bless Robin Hood! Robin Hood for ever!' shouted the crowd as they made way for the band of outlaws.

'I thank you, my dear master and friend,' said Scarlet as they went along. 'I did not think to see you here – nor that ever again I should tread the merry greenwood with you and our fellows and hear again the sweet music of the bow-strings and the woodman's horn.'

CHAPTER FIVE

HOW LITTLE JOHN CAME TO THE GREENWOOD

You gentlemen and yeomen good,
Come in and drink with Robin Hood;
If Robin Hood be not at home,
Come in and drink with Little John.

ANON: *Old Rhyme*

AFTER Robin Hood had rescued Will Scarlet from the Sheriff of Nottingham, he remained quietly in Sherwood Forest for some time, building huts in several of the most secret and hidden clearings, drilling his followers and teaching those who were new to it all the secrets of woodlore.

Many came to swell his band, outlaws, poor men who were suffering under cruel masters, and even a yeoman or two and several who had been forced into the service of the Sheriff or of various of the Norman knights and barons of the district.

The Great North Road passed through the Forest at that time, and surprise attacks supplied them with all they needed in the way of Lincoln green cloth and arrows – or the money with which to buy these.

When order and comfort had been brought to this new commonwealth of the greenwood, and precautions taken against surprise by the Sheriff or any of the neighbouring knights such as Sir Guy of Gisborne and their followers, Robin began to go further afield. He knew that it would be well to have several places of refuge

should Prince John send a large force to drive him out
of Sherwood, and in time he and his men were able to
disappear from the Nottingham district, and were often
to be found in Barnsdale, Yorkshire, or Plompton in
Cumberland: on occasion they were known even to visit
Pendle Forest in Lancashire and Delamere Forest in
Cheshire.

Much of their time was taken up in archery at which
all became very proficient, though none could ever
shoot so far or so true as Robin himself, and in fencing
with swords, or playing at quarterstaff. But there was
time for hunting as well, since venison was the most
usual food, varied with pork from the wild boars,
hares, and various wild fowl.

Many a time Robin would grow weary of the general
course of every day and wander off by himself, leaving
Will Scarlet in command. Often he returned from these
expeditions with news of a party of wealthy travellers to
be waylaid and robbed, or of some new injustice or
cruelty practised against a Saxon yeoman or Saxon
serfs. Sometimes he returned with a new member for his
band of outlaws – and the most noteworthy of these
chance meetings won for him the truest and most faithful of all his friends.

It was late in their first summer in Sherwood, and on
a sudden Robin grew restless.

'Stay you all here, my merry fellows,' he said early
one morning. 'But come and come swiftly if you hear
the blast on my horn that you all know as my special
call. We have had no sport these fourteen days and
more: no adventure has befallen us – so I will go forth
and seek for one. But if I should find myself in difficul-
ties, with no escape, then will I blow my horn.'

Then he bade farewell to Scarlet and the rest, and set
off blithely through the greenwood, his bow ready in his

hand, his eyes and ears alert for anything of danger or of interest.

About noon he came along a forest path to a wide, swiftly flowing stream which was crossed by a narrow bridge made of a single tree-trunk flattened on the top. As he approached it, he saw a tall yeoman hastening towards him beyond the stream.

'We cannot both cross at once, the bridge is too narrow,' thought Robin, and he quickened his pace meaning to be first over.

But the tall yeoman quickened his pace also, with the result that they each set foot on the opposite ends of the bridge at the same moment.

'Out of my way, little man!' shouted the stranger, who was a good foot taller than Robin. 'That is, unless you want a ducking in the stream!'

'Not so fast, not so fast, tall fellow,' answered Robin. 'Go you back until I have passed – or may be I will do the ducking!'

'Why then,' cried the stranger, waving his staff, 'I'll break your head first, and tip you into the water afterwards!'

'We'll see about that,' said Robin, and taking an arrow well feathered from the wing of a goose, he fitted it to the string.

'Draw that bow string ever so little!' shouted the stranger, 'and I'll first tan your hide with this good staff of mine, and then soak you well in the stream!'

'You talk like a plain ass!' exclaimed Robin scornfully, 'for were I to bend my bow I could send an arrow quite through your proud heart before you could touch me with your staff.'

'If I talk like an ass,' answered the stranger, 'you talk like a coward. You stand there well armed with a good

'I scorn to give way. Have at your head!'

long bow, while I have only a staff and am well out of your reach.'

'I scorn the name of coward,' cried Robin, slipping the arrow back into his quiver and unstringing his bow. 'Therefore will I lay aside my weapons and try your manhood with a quarter-staff such as your own – if you will but wait there until I cut one in the thicket.'

'Here I bide,' said the stranger cheerfully, 'one foot on the bridge – until you are ready for your cold bath in the stream!'

Robin Hood stepped aside to a thicket of trees and chose himself a stout six-foot staff of ground oak, straight and true and strong. Then he returned to the bridge, lopping and trimming his weapon as he came. He flung his bow and quiver on the bank, with his hood and his horn beside them, and set foot again on the bridge, crying merrily:

'Lo what a lusty staff I have, and a tough one at that – the very thing for knocking insolent rogues into the water! Let us fight here on the bridge, so that if one of us goes into the water, there will be no doubt who has won, and the victor may go on his way without a wetting.'

'With all my heart,' said the stranger. 'I scorn to give way. . . . Have at your head!' So saying, he grasped his staff one quarter of the way from the end, held his other hand ready to grasp it by the middle when using it as a shield, and advanced along the narrow bridge.

Robin came to meet him, flourishing his weapon round his head, and by a quick feint got the end in under his adversary's guard and made his ribs ring with the blow.

'This must be repaid!' cried the stranger. 'Be sure I'll give you as good as I get for so long as I am able to handle a staff – and I scorn to die in your debt when a good crack will pay what I owe!'

Then they went at it with mighty blows, rather as if threshing corn with flails. Presently the sharp rattle and clatter of wood upon wood was broken by a duller crack as the stranger struck Robin on the head, causing the blood to appear; and after that they lashed at each other all the more fiercely, Robin beating down the guard and getting in with blow after blow on shoulders and sides until the dust flew from the stranger's jerkin like smoke.

But on a sudden, with a great cry of rage the stranger whirled up his staff and smote so mightily and with such fury that even Robin could not withstand it, but tumbled head over heels into the stream and disappeared from sight.

'Good fellow, good fellow, where are you now?' shouted the stranger kneeling on the bridge and gazing anxiously down into the water.

'Here I am!' shouted Robin gaily as he pulled himself out by an overhanging hawthorn, 'just floating down the stream – and washing my bruised head as I go! I must acknowledge myself beaten: you're a fine fellow, and a good hitter – and as the day is yours, let there be no more battle between us.'

With that Robin picked up his horn and sounded a shrill blast on it. Then turning to the stranger he said:

'Whither were you hastening in the greenwood? I trust that you can spare time from your business to dine with me? Indeed I insist upon it – and must use force, if persuasion will not bring you!'

'To tell you truth,' answered the stranger, 'I was in search of a man they call Robin Hood –'

Before Robin could answer there was a crashing in the thicket and out bounded Will Scarlet, followed by many another of his men, making a bold show in their well-fitting doublets and hose of Lincoln Green.

'Good master!' cried Scarlet, 'what has befallen you that you blew the call for us? You are bleeding – and wet to the skin!'

'Nothing has befallen me,' answered Robin, 'save that this fine fellow here has just tumbled me into the stream with that long staff of his!'

'By the Rood,' exclaimed Scarlet, 'he cannot go scot free after so insulting bold Robin Hood. Come on, my merry men, let us give him a turn of the cold water.'

'No, no!' laughed Robin. 'He's a stout fellow, and tumbled me over in fair fight – so let him be. Come now, my friend,' he added, turning to the stranger, 'these bowmen will give you no cause for fear – they are all my friends. And they shall be your friends too, if you'll set your hand in mine and swear loyalty to Robin Hood and his companions. Speak up, jolly blade, and never fear – and we'll soon have you as fine a shot with the long bow as you are a player with the stout quarter-staff!'

'Why, here is my hand,' cried the stranger, 'and my heart goes with it, honest Robin. My name is John Little, and you need not fear that I will bring any shame upon you and your merry men: I am skilled in the arts of war and of the chase, and will follow you loyally wheresoever you may lead.'

'I still think you need a ducking!' said Scarlet, later that day as they all sat round a fire before which two plump does were roasting. 'But a good sprinkling with brown ale will at least do you no harm. It is our custom here in the greenwood to give every man who joins us a new name. What say you, my friends, shall we not make this into a christening feast for our new friend, and bestow a greenwood name upon him?'

'Well said, good Scarlet!' cried the outlaws, gathering round in a ring of laughing faces. 'And Robin shall be his godfather!'

'Agreed!' smiled Robin. 'Now to your work, good Parson Scarlet!'

'Why then,' cried Scarlet, filling a gigantic mug with foaming ale, 'attend all of you! This child, this babe brought here for christening, was called John Little. But seeing that he is so small, so puny a babe – being indeed no more than seven foot high, and a mere ell or so about the waist (what say you, child, a mere yard and no yard and a quarter? – well, well, a year of venison and strong ale will make you two yards about!) – As I was saying, seeing that the child is so under size –'

'And still under-nourished!' interrupted John Little, sniffing hungrily in the direction of the steaming venison.

'Seeing all this!' continued Scarlet serenely, 'we'll turn him back to front – and name him Little John now and for ever. Long live Little John!'

With that he made as if to pour the ale over his god-child's head, but Little John twisted the mug out of his hand, and shouting aloud: 'Thus Little John pledges Robin Hood and all who follow him in the merry green-wood!' he set the great tankard to his lips and drained it at a draught.

After that, they feasted and rejoiced far into the evening. But thence forward Little John became one of Robin's most faithful followers and truest friends, and in time, as Will Scarlet grew too old for such active service, he became his second in command.

But though he grew no shorter, and certainly no narrower round the waist, the name of Little John stuck to him, nor was he ever known by any other.

CHAPTER SIX

HOW SIR RICHARD OF LEGH
PAID THE ABBOT

My londes beth set to wedde, Robyn,
Untyll a certayne daye,
To a ryche abbot here besyde,
Of Saynt Mary abbay.
ANON: *A Lytell Geste of Robyn Hode* (1489)

ONE day, soon after he came to the greenwood, Little John was wandering with Robin Hood deep in the wilds of Barnsdale. With them were Scarlet and Much, besides a small party of picked bowmen, and they were in search of a hidden site in which to make a camp to which the whole band could retire if Sherwood should prove too dangerous at any time.

When a place was found and the camp was being made, Little John said to Robin:

'Good master, let us shoot a fat deer for our dinner: we should be all the better for a feast!'

'I have no great desire to dine just yet,' said Robin, 'and there is still time to find us a guest for dinner. Do you and Scarlet and Much take bow in hand and go through the woods to the Great North Road which runs not far from here. Wait there in hiding until some uninvited guest passes that way – and bring him to dinner whether he will or no.'

'What kind of guest would you have?' asked Little John who was still unused to Robin's ways.

'Well,' laughed Robin, 'some bold baron, bishop or

abbot will pay best for his dinner, or even a proud
knight or squire. But look you hinder no honest yeoman
nor labouring man, nor set upon any company if there
be a woman in it of good and virtuous mien.'

Away went Little John with his two companions and
were soon in hiding beside the road. At first there was
no sign of any likely man, but at length a knight came
riding slowly from the direction of York, his hood hanging over his eyes, and his chin sunk sorrowfully on his
chest.

Then Little John stepped out into the road and bowed
low before him, catching his horse's bridle in one hand
as he did so.

'Welcome, gentle knight,' he said. 'To me you are
very welcome. I come with an invitation for you from
my master, who waits fasting – as I and my two companions wait also - until you are set at dinner with us.'

'What master is yours?' asked the knight.

'Robin Hood!' answered Little John.

'A noble and a gentle master,' said the knight. 'I have
heard tell of him, and right gladly will I be his guest.'

So away they went into the greenwood, and at the
camp in Barnsdale, Robin greeted the knight full
courteously.

'Welcome, sir knight,' he cried, 'welcome you are
indeed. I have fasted three hours in the hope of your
company!'

'God save you, good Robin Hood,' murmured the
knight, 'and all your merry men too. I will indeed eat my
dinner with you - though little appetite have I this day.'

Then, having washed in fair water, and uncovered
while Robin said grace, they sat down to a fine meal of
venison, with swan and pheasant as side dishes, and
many another delicacy with which skilful shooting had
provided them.

'I thank you,' said the knight when the meal was ended. 'I have not dined so well these past three weeks. If I come this way again, mayhap I can ask you to dine with me – but there is poor chance of it now.' And the knight sighed sadly.

'Many thanks, kind sir,' answered Robin. 'But now, before you go, I must ask you to pay something towards what you have eaten: the tithe of the forest, we call it. I am but a poor yeoman now, and it has never been good manners to let a yeoman pay for a knight's dinner.'

'Alas,' said his guest, sighing even more deeply, 'my coffers are empty; there is nought that I can proffer without shame.'

'Search his saddle bags, Little John,' commanded Robin. 'You must not blame us, sir,' he added to the knight, 'it is our custom. But tell me truly how much you have.'

'No more than ten shillings,' was the answer.

'If you have indeed no more,' said Robin, 'I will not touch a single penny of it – and if you have need of more, why more will I lend to you.'

'Here,' called out Little John, who had spread a mantle on the ground and emptied the knight's bags on to it, 'here I find but half a pound and no more.'

'The knight is a true man, then,' said Robin. 'Fill him now a cup of good wine, and he may be gone if he will, or stay and tell us his story. For indeed I wonder to see how thin and old his clothes are, and how sad and weary he looks. Sir knight, tell me how this comes about: have you spent all or gambled all away? Did you lose money in usury, or spend it upon women – or has it been stolen from you?'

'By God that made me,' said the knight, 'my wealth was lost by no evil of my doing. My ancestors have been knights this hundred years and more; we held fair lands in Cheshire – four hundred pounds had I to spend in every year, and no name was held in greater honour than that of Sir Richard of Legh. But now I have no goods, save my wife and young children – and they are like to starve.'

'In what manner, noble Sir Richard, have you lost all this?' asked Robin.

'By the cruel craft and usury of the Abbot of St Mary's hard by here,' answered Sir Richard. 'My son set out with King Richard to the Holy Land – and news came but lately that he lay a prisoner, and I must raise a thousand pounds for his ransom, and that right speedily. Six hundred was all that I could come by, till the Abbot lent to me four hundred on the surety of my house and lands: tomorrow is the day that my bond to him falls due. If I do not pay him the four hundred pounds by noon, both house and lands are his. And I have but ten shillings, for I can beg or borrow no more – and what I had raised Prince John's tax gatherers came three weeks ago and took from me. May be they did so at the prompting of the Abbot who, as I know well, longs to take all my lands.'

'What sum do you owe?' asked Robin. 'Tell me as exactly as you can.'

'Just four hundred pounds,' answered Sir Richard.

'And if you do not pay it tomorrow?'

'Why then, I lose my lands, and there is nought for me to do but to go overseas and serve the King in Palestine. It would be a sight to have seen, ere I die, where Our Lord lived and died as a Man, and to have stricken a blow towards freeing His Holy Sepulchre from the unbelieving Saracens; but woe is me for my wife and small children, and for the land which was my father's before me and which I had hoped would be my son's and his heirs' for ever.'

'Have you no friends who can lend you the money?' asked Robin.

'Never a one will own me now, though they were kind enough when I was rich and prosperous,' sighed Sir Richard. 'But now the only surety I can offer for a loan is my word as a knight, and my faith by Our Lady the Holy Mother of Christ.'

'And no better faith could a man have,' exclaimed Robin, crossing himself devoutly.

'Go now to our treasury, Little John, and see if you can there find four hundred pounds. And see also what we can do for clothes such as a knight should wear. And this day twelve-month doubtless he will seek us out in the greenwood and tell us how he fares and what he can give to us in return.'

'Now may God bless you, kind Robin Hood,' said Sir Richard. 'And be sure that this day twelve-month will find me once again in your company.' ...

The time was drawing towards noon next day, and the Abbot of St Mary's sat in great state in his abbey, with his monks about him, receiving payments of rents from the many tenants who held lands and houses from him.

Most of the rents or debts were paid early in the morning: in a few cases the tenant or the borrower was unable to pay – and then the Abbot rubbed his hands and smiled a fat, contented smile, while his Prior entered a new possession among the Abbey's holdings.

'My lord, there is still the debt of Sir Richard of Legh,' said the Prior when all else had been paid or settled. 'Four hundred pounds did we lend to him, and he vowed to pay it, even to the last penny, by noon today – or else forfeit his fair lands at Legh in Cheshire.'

The Abbot rubbed his hands. 'Many a rich acre!' he

chuckled. 'And the fine house of Legh Hall! All ours, all ours!'

'My lord, it wants still half an hour of noon,' the Prior reminded him.

'Tush, tush!' gurgled the Abbot. 'Sir Richard cannot pay! Prince John sent the tax gatherers to him but last month – oh, I have it on sure authority that Sir Richard cannot pay – my good friend Sir Guy of Gisborne saw to that, ha! ha!'

'Yet we must wait until noon,' said the Prior.

'Ah well,' murmured the Abbot, 'but a little while – and then all is ours.' At that moment a monk came swiftly to them.

'Sir Richard is here!' he whispered to the Abbot, 'but in poor array: you need not fear that he can pay his debt!'

Sure enough, Sir Richard came slowly up the hall to where the Abbot sat, and he looked sad enough, and poor enough too in the old and tattered cloak which was wrapped about him. He came before the table at which sat the Abbot with his Prior and his Justice, and knelt down humbly.

'God's blessing, my lord Abbot,' he said. 'I am here upon my hour.'

'Have you brought the money you owe me?' was all that the Abbot could gasp out.

'Not one penny,' sighed Sir Richard, and hung his head.

'Indeed, you are a sorry debtor!' cried the Abbot with a great sigh of relief, and then turning to the Justice, he exclaimed: 'Drink to me, my friend! Wish me luck, good sirs!

'But what do you here?' he added, turning quickly back to Sir Richard. 'If you have not brought my money back, why have you come at all?'

'To beg for longer grace,' answered Sir Richard
humbly. 'Bethink you, my lord Abbot – my son is
prisoner to the wicked Saracens: he was taken fighting
at good King Richard's side, and for the benefit of Holy
Church. Surely Holy Church will grant me but six
months more to clear the debt – which I can do in that
time.'

'You must pay or forfeit'

'No, no,' broke in the Justice. 'Your time is up. You
must pay or forfeit!'

'Now, good Father Prior,' begged Sir Richard, 'stand
you my friend and beg grace of the Abbot!'

'Nay, not I!' cried the Prior.

'Then, my lord Abbot,' pleaded Sir Richard, 'at
least hold my land in trust until I have found the
money, and I will be your true servant and serve you
faithfully.'

'No, by God!' shouted the Abbot. 'You get no further help from me, false, perjured knight that would
cheat Holy Church of four hundred pounds. Get you
gone out of my Abbey, ere I bid my serving men whip
you from the door like a stray cur!'

'You lie, Abbot!' cried Sir Richard, drawing himself
up suddenly. 'I am no false knight! But for you, a servant of God, to suffer a knight to kneel before you and
beg your charity – you are shamed for ever!'

'Get hence!' shouted the Abbot, purple with rage.
'Your lands and houses are mine! Hark – the clock
strikes twelve!'

'The clock strikes twelve,' said Sir Richard quietly,
'and I have paid my debt!'

As he spoke, he flung back his cloak, showing that he
was well and richly clad beneath it. Then he laid four
leather bags on the table in front of the Abbot, and
stood silent.

The Abbot's jaw dropped and the colour fled from his
face.

'Count the money,' he said in a shaking voice. The
Prior did so, and found it exact.

'Now,' said Sir Richard, 'the land is mine again, and
all the cruel Abbots in England cannot prove otherwise!'

With that he strode from the Abbey, while the Abbot
stood and cursed him, threatening vengeance when the
time should come.

But Sir Richard rode full speed to Legh Hall where
his wife was waiting anxiously for him.

'Be merry, good lady!' he cried. 'All is saved – I am
free from the Abbot. We have but to dwell quietly at
home for a year, and I can save enough to pay back kind
Robin Hood who lent me the money.'

'And I will pray for Robin Hood,' said the Lady of
Legh.

CHAPTER SEVEN

MAID MARIAN OF SHERWOOD FOREST

Why, she is called Maid Marion, honest friend,
Because she lives a spotless maiden life;
And shall, till Robin's outlaw life have end,
That he may lawfully take her to wife;
Which, if King Richard come, will not be long.

ANTHONY MUNDAY: *The Downfall of Robert*
Earl of Huntingdon (1601)

GAMWELL HALL, seat of Robin Hood's uncle Sir William Gamwell, was not far from Nottingham, and thither Sir Guy of Gisborne rode one day attended only by his squire.

Sir William welcomed Sir Guy, and after feasting him well, suggested that he should come with him next day to the great Gamwell festival held not far away in the forest.

Hoping to find out where Robin Hood was, Sir Guy agreed readily to this. But of course he said no word of his real reasons either to Sir William or to young Will Gamwell who rode with him.

It was a merry scene in the green glade of the forest: young men and girls dancing round the Maypole, barrels of ale broached for Sir William's tenants, and many a game or contest for young and old alike.

Sir Guy sat quietly under a tree with old Sir William watching it all, and only once did he lean forward suddenly with an angry glint in his eyes, and that was when young Will Gamwell led out one of the maidens to dance whom he recognized suddenly as the Lady Marian Fitzwalter disguised as a peasant girl.

'What maiden is she who dances with your son?' asked Sir Guy.

'That?' answered Sir William vaguely. 'Oh, she is known as the shepherdess Clorinda: she is often at these feasts, but really I can tell you little of her!'

'You mean you won't tell me!' thought Sir Guy as his host hastily changed the conversation. 'I am certainly on the right trail now!'

Later in the day came a band of foresters in Lincoln green and there was a great contest of archery in which 'Clorinda' took part as well and seemed as good an archer as any of them.

Sir Guy mounted his horse and rode casually down to the butts to watch the sport. As he drew near, Clorinda discharged her arrow, and a cheer went up from all who were watching since she had shot it into the very centre of the gold, which was the middle ring of the target.

'I must needs shoot well indeed to equal that, fair Clorinda,' said the chief of the foresters stepping forward and setting an arrow to his string. The arrow sped, and another cheer arose, for everyone could see that it too had struck within the ring of gold, so close to that of Clorinda that the points were in contact and the feathers were intermingled.

'I claim your hand, fair Queen of the May,' said the forester bowing low before Clordina, and with a blush and a smile she held out her hand to him and he led her away into the dance.

But Sir Guy had recognized the forester, and now he turned to Will Gamwell who stood beside him.

'What is that archer's name?' he asked.

'Robin, I believe,' said young Gamwell carelessly. 'I think they call him Robin!'

'Is that all you know of him?'

'What more is there to know?'

'Why, let me tell you,' said Sir Guy sternly, 'that he is none other than the outlawed Robert Fitzooth, called Earl of Huntingdon; and there is a large reward offered to any man who can bring him prisoner before the Sheriff of Nottingham.'

'Is he really?' said Will Gamwell, as if not in the least interested.

'He would be a prize well worth taking.'

'I expect so.'

'Shall we not take him then?'

'You may if you please.'

'But are your tenants and followers not loyal?'

'Loyal they are indeed!'

'Then,' exclaimed Sir Guy, growing more and more angry, 'if I were to call upon them in the King's name, would they not aid and assist?'

'Assuredly they would,' answered Gamwell, 'on one side or the other!'

'But I have Prince John's warrant for the arrest of Fitzooth,' said Sir Guy. 'What would you then advise me to do?'

'Why,' answered Gamwell calmly, 'I would advise you to turn round and ride your hardest for Nottingham – unless you want a volley of arrows, a shower of stones and a hailstorm of cudgel-blows to help you on your way!'

On hearing this, Sir Guy's squire clapped spurs to his horse and went away at full gallop – which gave Sir Guy an excuse for galloping away after him shouting:

'Stop, you rascal!' until they were out of sight of the Gamwell gathering.

They did not draw rein then, however, but made all speed to Nottingham where Sir Guy roused the Sheriff with the news that Robin Hood was within a few miles with scarcely a dozen men.

Within half an hour he was off again, accompanied by the Sheriff and an armed band, hurrying along the road towards Gamwell.

The sun was sinking as they came to a bridge across the river and on the further side saw a small party of foresters and men at arms headed by the shepherdess Clorinda who still carried her bow, and by whose side now walked the gigantic form of Brother Michael Tuck, lately of Fountains Abbey.

'Now who be these that come riding so fast this way?' bellowed the Friar. 'False traitors all, I'll be bound – yes, there I perceive Sir Guy of Gisborne to whom the sacred dues of hospitality are unknown, and with him the Sheriff of Nottingham – loyal servant of whoever pays him the fattest fees!'

'Out of the way, renegade Friar!' shouted Sir Guy angrily, for the Friar and his party had reached the bridge first. 'And you, Lady Marian, hasten away to Arlingford, for you are in truly doubtful and traitorous company.'

'You mistake, false knight, you mistake!' declared the Friar calmly. 'The lady here is the fair Clorinda, well known throughout the forest of Sherwood as the Queen of the Shepherdesses. As for the doubtful and traitorous company – I see none of it on *this* side of the bridge!'

'Out of the way!' echoed the Sheriff angrily. 'We seek Robert Fitzooth, known as Robin Hood, who but an hour since was consorting with you not far from this spot!'

'By the Rood, you'll not pass this way,' bellowed the Friar, 'until you have made full apology to the fair Clorinda and myself for all terms, taunts, and other words of slander uttered in the hearing of these good fellows!'

Roaring lustily, the great Friar stood there whirling **his staff**

'Force them aside!' cried Sir Guy impatiently. 'Robin Hood is escaping us even now! And catch that froward girl for me: Lord Fitzwalter will reward me well when I bring her back to him!'

Sir Guy raised his hand derisively as he spoke, and swift as thought Clorinda raised her bow, the string hummed, and Sir Guy's hand was transfixed by an arrow.

'Treachery! Cut them down!' shouted the Sheriff. The bow-string hummed again, the Sheriff's horse reared up as an arrow whizzed into the ground between its forefeet, and the Sheriff fell backwards out of the saddle and sat heavily down in a large pool of mud.

Thereupon arrows sped amongst the Sheriff's men, who rushed up the steep bridge, only to be beaten back by the mighty staff in the hands of the great Friar. For, roaring lustily, he stood there alone, whirling his staff from side to side among the Sheriff's men, knocking down one, breaking the ribs of another, dislocating the shoulder of a third, flattening the nose of a fourth, cracking the skull of a fifth, and pitching a sixth into the river, until the few who were lucky enough to escape with whole bones clapped spurs to their horses and fled for their lives – the outraged Sheriff leading the way, and the wounded Sir Guy of Gisborne bringing up the rear, amidst the laughter of the fair 'Clorinda' and her followers and the jeers and taunts of the Friar.

Next morning Lord Fitzwalter was disturbed over his breakfast by the loud blast of a trumpet and the sounds of a general alarm. Hastening to the castle gate, he saw a large body of armed men drawn up on the further side of the moat, with a herald blowing a trumpet and an officer bidding them 'Lower the drawbridge, in the King's name!'

'What for, in the devil's name?' roared Lord Fitz-walter angrily.

'Be it known to all just men!' proclaimed the herald, 'that the Sheriff of Nottingham lies in bed grievously bruised, many of his men are like to die of divers injuries and the good knight Sir Guy of Gisborne is sorely wounded by an arrow. And we charge Sir William Gamwell, the Lady Marian Fitzwalter and one Friar Michael lately of Fountains Abbey, as agents and accomplices in the said riot, and traitors for that they have aided and consorted with the outlaw Robin Hood, otherwise Robert Fitzooth sometime of Locksley Hall.'

'Agents and accomplices!' spluttered Lord Fitz-walter. 'What do you mean by coming here with this nonsensical story of my daughter the Lady Marian bruising the Sheriff, injuring his men and shooting arrows into Sir Guy of Gisborne! Off you go, or I'll bid my men shoot at you with their cross bows!'

'You will hear more of this!' shouted the officer in command of the troop. 'Not so lightly may you flout the will of our liege lord Prince John!'

'Then let him come in person,' shouted Lord Fitz-walter, 'or send someone whom I can trust. How know I that you are not some of these very Sherwood outlaws in disguise, trying to gain entrance to my castle under cover of the King's name and a silly story about my girl bruising sheriffs and shooting men-at-arms!'

The troop of men, seeing that an archer with a cross-bow stood ready at every loop-hole, that the draw-bridge was up, and the moat both wide and deep, retreated with many threats in the direction of Notting-ham.

Lord Fitzwalter at once summoned his daughter, and on demanding the truth, Marian confessed that she was known in the Forest as the shepherdess Clorinda, and told the story of Sir Guy's defeat at Gamwell bridge.

'You go no more forth from the castle!' declared Lord Fitzwalter.

'Then I get out if I can,' answered Marian firmly, 'and am under no obligation to return.'

'Away with you to the topmost turret chamber!' ordered her father. 'No one will get you out of there!'

'Prince John will do so,' said Marian, with a shudder. 'I hear that he is now at Nottingham – those were his men before the castle even now. He saw me on the eve of my wedding to Robin of Locksley, and it is said that he has sworn to take me – and perhaps not hand me over to Sir Guy as readily as he has promised.'

'I'll defy a wicked Prince as surely as a wicked knight,' shouted Lord Fitzwalter.

'You cannot withstand Prince John,' said Marian. 'Think of the power he can command. He'll sack the castle, hang you from the nearest tree – and take me whether you will or no. . . . But if you shut me up – and I escape from the castle, no blame can be attached to you, and you can welcome him here with every sign of regret, for my absence and fury at my flight.'

'Hum! Ha!' Lord Fitzwalter opened his mouth to swear, but shut it again as he realized the truth of what Marian said.

'Then if you – er – escape,' he asked, 'do you go to Sherwood Forest as half wife of this outlaw Robin Hood?'

'I go to Robin Hood,' answered Marian quietly, 'but until King Richard returns from Palestine, pardons him and restores him to his rightful position, I dwell in Sherwood Forest as Maid Marian – promised but not united to Robin. And this he has sworn by God and Our Lady, and here and now I re-affirm the oath.'

Lord Fitzwalter thought for a few minutes.

'Robin or Robert, he's a true and honourable man,' he said at last. 'And you are my daughter, and would bring no dishonour upon our line. . . . God bless you, Marian. . . . Go to your room now – and do not let anyone see you leaving Arlingford Castle, or it will be the worse for us all!'

When, a few hours later, Prince John rode up at the head of a hundred men, Lord Fitzwalter met him at the gate with the most profuse expressions of loyalty, begged pardon for his behaviour to the herald in the morning, and placed the whole castle at his disposal.

'I am honoured, deeply honoured, your Royal Highness,' he said, still on his knees. 'There is no guest more welcome than yourself – and your trusty followers. Had you but sent sure proof with your herald this morning, I had admitted him at once: but with this cursed outlaw Robin Hood so nearby, one must be careful. Why, he came in disguise into Nottingham itself and rescued one of his ruffians from the very foot of the gallows!'

Prince John was graciously pleased to accept Lord Fitzwalter's apologies, and his hospitality at the same time. But when he asked to be presented to the Lady Marian, it was found that she was no longer in her room.

Then Lord Fitzwalter raged round the castle, cursing the carelessness of his followers and threatening dreadful things to the guards who had let her pass. But nothing could be learned of her whereabouts, though one guard volunteered the information that a young archer had been seen standing in the gatehouse an hour or so before Prince John's arrival – and that youth was missing also.

Prince John graciously lent half his followers to Lord Fitzwalter, and they scoured the neighbourhood for several days. But the Lady Marian Fitzwalter had vanished.

Hearing that Prince John was at Nottingham with a whole troop of his followers, Robin Hood walked near the edge of Sherwood disguised as a Forest Ranger. He hoped to meet some traveller coming from Nottingham, fall into conversation with him, and learn of Prince John's movements or intentions.

Presently, as he strolled along the road, he met a young man dressed in forest attire who held a bow in his hand, carried a good quiver of arrows on his back and wore a stout broadsword at his side.

'How now, good fellow!' cried Robin in a harsh voice. 'Whither away so fast? What news is there today in the good city of Nottingham?'

'I go about my own business,' replied the young man, 'and the news is that Prince John has come to Nottingham to put down the outlaws in the forest.'

'About time, too,' said Robin, remembering that he was posing as a Ranger, or keeper of the Royal Deer. 'And what do you, my fine lad, with that long bow and those goodly arrows?'

'I mind my own business,' answered the youth, 'which I would that other wanderers in Sherwood did likewise!'

'My business is with such as you,' said Robin sternly. 'Tell me your name and business, or my sword must enforce it.'

'Two can play at that game,' cried the youth, and flinging down his bow and quiver, he drew his sword and stood on the defence. Robin did likewise, and a minute later the blades clashed together.

Very soon Robin found that his antagonist was at least his match in all the skill and practice of swordsmanship, though weaker in the wrist than he, and not so heavy in the sheer weight of blows.

They fought for some time without either gaining

much vantage, though the blood was running down Robin's face, and his antagonist was wounded in the arm.

'Hold your hand, good fellow – let us fight no more,' said Robin at last, stepping back and leaning on his sword, quite forgetful of his pretended role as Forest Ranger. 'You fight too well to be wasted like this: come, throw in your lot with Robin Hood and be one of his merry men.'

'Are you Robin Hood?' gasped the youth.

'Robin Hood I am, and no other!' was the reply.

'Oh, Robin, Robin! Do you not know me?' cried his late antagonist with a sudden change of voice.

'Marian!' gasped Robin. 'And I wounded you, and knew you not!' In another moment his arms were around her.

'Welcome to Sherwood,' he said at length, when she had poured out all her tale to him. 'Come away with me now to our secret glen, and let Scarlet and Much, Little John, and the rest, welcome their queen – as I do; and swear, as I do, to be true and faithful servants now and henceforward to you, Maid Marian of Sherwood Forest.'

There was feasting and rejoicing that night in the secret glade where Robin and his merry men did honour to their lovely queen. There was no lack of good roasted venison, great flagons of wine were set on the board, bowls of brown ale, and many another delicacy.

When the feast was ended, Robin rose with a great flagon in his hand.

'My friends!' he cried. 'Let us drink first, now as ever, to King Richard – King Richard and his speedy return from the Crusade!'

When the pledge was drunk, Robin rose again.

'And now!' he cried, 'drink to our Maiden Queen!

To the Lady Marian! Let us pledge ourselves once more to the true service of God and His Holy Mother, as true Christian men should. But let us also, even as true knights to their lady, pledge ourselves that all our actions shall be so pure and so far from all evil that we do nothing we should think shame of were it done in the presence of our queen, our Maid Marian!'

'Maid Marian of Sherwood Forest!' cried every man there, springing to their feet. 'To our King and Queen of the Forest – to Robin Hood and Maid Marian!'

CHAPTER EIGHT

THE COMING OF FRIAR TUCK

And here's a grey friar, good as heart can desire,
To absolve all our sins as the case may require:
Who with courage so stout lays his oak plant about,
And puts to the rout all the foes of his choir:
For we are his choristers, we merry foresters,
Chorusing thus with our militant friar.

THOMAS LOVE PEACOCK: *Maid Marian* (*1822*)

SUMMER had come and gone, and the leaves were turning brown in Sherwood, when on a day as Little John and Scarlet and the pick of Robin's men practised archery and quarter-staff in the secret glade, Marian said suddenly:

'Robin, it grieves and surprises me that we have heard nothing of good Brother Michael.'

Robin nodded thoughtfully. 'He surely knows that you dwell now in the forest,' he said, 'for he did you good service on the day of the Gamwell feast when Guy of Gisborne and the Sheriff tried to take me.'

'That was indeed a strange encounter,' Marian remarked. 'He came suddenly along the river bank waving his mighty staff – and disappeared as suddenly after the fray, without speaking a word to me.'

'Your father forbade him to visit you at Arlingford?' queried Robin.

Marian nodded. 'And the Abbot of Fountains Abbey cast him out also,' she added. 'He said he would live a hermit in some cell by the river, as plain Friar Tuck.'

Robin thought for a little while, and then with an exclamation he called Will Scarlet to him:

'Scarlet, what was it you were saying not many days since of a hermit living in the cell at Copmanhurst?'

'He's a mighty man,' said Scarlet, 'who looks far too well fed – and well drunk also – to be a hermit. But he dwells there all alone by the river, and for a penance he carries any traveller across the river at the ford there – though I doubt not but that he asks a good fee for his ferrying. It is said also that he will fight, on a challenge, with the quarter staff, and crack the crown of any man who dares stand against him.'

'Now!' cried Robin, 'I swear by the Virgin that I will go tomorrow and seek out this hermit. If he prove to be Michael Tuck, so much the better, and if not we will at least have a round at crown-cracking. If he be a good fellow, and a virtuous priest as well, we would be the gainers by his presence amongst us here in the forest.'

Next morning accordingly Robin disguised himself as a wandering minstrel, though without forsaking either bow or sword, and set out through the forest in the direction of Gamwell.

He turned aside when he came to the river and followed it for some time until he came to the ford of Copmanhurst. And there sure enough was a boat moored to the further side, while a wisp of smoke rising among the rocks showed that the hermitage built against the cliff edge was inhabited.

'Ho-la! good ferryman! Ho, there!' shouted Robin.

'Who calls?' answered a deep voice, and a gigantic friar strode out upon the river bank. He was dressed in a brown robe such as all friars wore, but it was well girdled about with a curtal of cord at which hung a huge broad-sword. On his head, in place of a hood, the friar wore a round steel head-piece, while the sleeves rolled back showed great muscular arms far better suited to a warrior than a priest.

'Now then, my fine fellow!' shouted Robin, 'come and ferry me over the river!'

'All in good time, my son, all in good time!' boomed the friar, and seizing a mighty staff he stepped into the boat and poled it across to where Robin stood.

'A mere minstrel!' he grumbled as Robin stepped aboard. 'He could have swum it – and the wetting would have done him good. Alas for my vow!'

When they reached the other side the friar sprang quickly on shore and turned to his passenger.

'Now then,' he cried, 'let me see how your purse is lined!'

'Surely, good hermit,' said Robin mildly, 'you would not turn robber?'

'Not so,' answered the friar, 'I do but ask for alms – as is the Church's due!'

'No man is compelled to give alms,' Robin reminded him, 'save only by his conscience.'

'A good doctrine,' agreed the friar, 'but the office of a priest is to awake the conscience – which I will now proceed to do with my good staff across your shoulders – unless your conscience should be awake already!'

'Come then and search my purse,' said Robin, pretending to cringe in fear. The friar dropped his staff and advanced unsuspectingly, and Robin suddenly whipped out his sword and held it to the friar's throat.

'For that, base hermit,' he cried, 'you shall carry me across the river once more – and this time it shall be upon your back! And no fee shall you receive for so doing, save a cracked sconce, if you again demand any.'

'A bargain,' said the friar calmly, 'for the water is low, the labour is light – and the fee such a one as I relish!'

The friar bent down and Robin, still with the drawn
sword in his hand, mounted on his back. Walking as if
he took no note of his burden, the friar strode down into
the water and made his way across by the ford until he
had brought Robin safe and dry to the other bank.

Here, however, he pitched him to the ground so suddenly that he was forced to drop his sword to save himself from falling.

'Now then, my fine fellow,' said the friar, setting his
foot on Robin's blade and drawing his own as he spoke,
'you must carry me back across the river – and I'll
crack your sconce in payment when we get to the other
side.'

'Turn and turn about!' cried Robin cheerfully, and
he bent his back and took up the enormous weight of the
friar. It was hard labour indeed, even for so strong a
man as Robin, for the friar must have weighed nearly
twenty stone; but he carried him down to the river and
waded slowly and carefully into the middle of the stream.

'A good mount, truly!' crowed the fat friar, chuckling
to himself at Robin's exertions. 'This puts me in mind
of a fable writ by the learned Aesop of the two simple-
tons who carried their ass home from the market town!'

'Yes,' panted Robin. 'But it reminds me more of
another fable – that of the ass with the bags of salt. That
was a better example, and a wiser – or so it seems to me.'

And as he said this, Robin gave a sudden dextrous
jerk and flung the friar over his head into the deepest
part of the river. Then he sprang hastily to the bank and
turned back to laugh heartily at the great fat figure
floundering and blowing like a whale in the water his
bald scalp covered in green slime and chickweed.

'Fine fellow, fine fellow!' spluttered the friar scram-
bling to shore at length. 'Make ready now and I will
pay you the cracked sconce I owe you!'

'No, no!' laughed Robin. 'I have not earned it. But you have earned it, and you alone shall have it.'

After that they set at one another with great staves, smiting and feinting and raining blows like two lusty farmers threshing the corn.

Robin gave a sudden dextrous jerk and flung
the friar over his head

At last they paused through sheer weariness – and though neither was beaten, both had paid the toll of a broken sconce.

'Honour, methinks, is satisfied!' puffed the friar. 'Let us shake hands and part friends. You are a stout fellow for a minstrel, by the rood!'

'I have used sword as well as harp,' answered Robin.

'But never have I met with such a wielder of the cudgel as you are. So a truce to our quarrel, and come let us rest a while in your cell – where, doubtless, you can set food and drink before a poor wanderer.'

'Alas,' said the friar, looking suddenly meek and pious. 'There is no food here fit for a man such as yourself. You are welcome to share the frugal diet of a poor hermit vowed to fasting and prayer.'

With that he led Robin to the hermitage, which was no more than a rough hut of stone and wood with a thatched roof, built across the front of a cave in the low cliff which fringed the river at that point.

Inside were but a table, a couple of stools, a crucifix hanging on the wall, and a bed of leaves and dried grass at the back of the shallow cave. The friar reached down a dish of pease from a shelf of rock, set it on the table, and poured water out of a jug into a couple of drinking horns.

'It seems, holy brother,' said Robin, seating himself on a stool and sampling a mouthful of the pease without much enjoyment – 'It seems that a few pease and a jug of water have thriven you marvellously. Surely it is a miracle when a man who lives upon a handful of pease is yet round and red-faced – and as lusty a fighter as you have shown yourself to be!'

'Ah, good minstrel,' answered the friar with a deep sigh, 'it has pleased Our Lady and my patron saint, the holy Dunstan, to bless exceedingly the pittance to which I restrain myself.'

'Aye, but there is no such blessing granted to poor wayfarers like myself,' said Robin. 'Surely some kindly forest ranger visits you from time to time and leaves some store for the use of travellers – which they are doubtless as ready as I am to pay for in other coin than the ferry fee!'

So saying he flung a piece of gold on the table, and eyed the friar with a merry twinkle in his eye. The friar looked at the coin hungrily, hummed and hawed for a while, and then going to the side of the cave opened a cupboard cunningly concealed in the rock and drew out an enormous venison pasty. He set it on the board, and Robin set to work to satisfy his hunger at such a speed that the pasty began visibly to shrink.

The friar sat watching him, his face growing longer and longer as the pasty grew shorter and shorter, until at last Robin took pity on him and exclaimed:

'Good friar, far be it from me to tempt you into breaking your vows of abstinence, but surely good manners demand that a host should partake of the same dish as his guest – if only to show that the dish is wholesome and harmless!'

'By the rood!' cried the friar, his eyes lighting up. 'Long sojourn alone in a hermit cell had make me forget that excellent rule! A thousand apologies, my worthy guest.'

With that he set to work on the other end of the pasty – cramming in two mouthfuls for every one that Robin could take – and before long the dish was empty.

'Holy man,' said Robin gravely, 'I'll wager another piece of gold that the same forester who left that pasty here for the good cheer of travellers, left also a stoop of wine for their further refreshment! I think that if you were to search your cupboard again, you would find that I was right.'

The friar rose to his feet with a broad grin – which he tried in vain to transform into a look of pious reproach – and set before his guest a leathern bottle containing at least a gallon. From this he filled the two horns, and then said:

'Sir stranger, pledge me in this, and as, in duty bound
– tell me your name.'

'Right willingly,' answered Robin, 'but once again
you forget that you are my host, and a man must know
the name of his bounteous entertainer.'

'I am but the plain Hermit of Copmanhurst,' was the
answer, 'and my name is Friar Tuck!'

'Then, good Friar Tuck!' cried Robin. 'Good Brother
Michael that was, I drink to you – I Robin Hood,
who once also had another name. Waes hael, Friar
Tuck!'

'Drink hael, Robin Hood!' answered Friar Tuck,
draining his horn at a single draught. 'Right glad am I
that the minstrel should hide so good a man.'

'Come back to Sherwood with me, jolly Friar,'
begged Robin. 'I have come hither to seek you, with a
summons from the Lady Marian, whose confessor you
were. Truly, when you broke my head with your staff
I guessed you were the man I sought – but when you
made such short work of the venison pasty, I knew that
I was right!'

'With all my heart!' bellowed Friar Tuck, pouring
out another horn full of wine. 'Farewell to pease and
spring-water! You live well in the forest, jolly Robin, or
so it is said. That you need a priest there is no shadow
of doubt: and that I am the priest you need, no one will
dare to deny!'

Robin meanwhile had stepped to the door of the
hermitage and sounded the call to his men.

'Drink another draught before we go!' shouted Friar
Tuck. 'It would be a sad pity to leave behind so good a
wine. Here's to you, Robin Hood; and here's to our life
in merry Sherwood!'

And with that he drained another horn, and sang
right lustily:

THE COMING OF FRIAR TUCK

Oh, bold Robin Hood is a forester good,
As ever drew bow in the merry greenwood:
At his bugle's shrill singing the echoes are ringing,
The wild deer are springing for many a rood:
Its summons we follow, through brake, over hollow,
The thrice-blown shrill summons of bold Robin Hood!

CHAPTER NINE

HOW SIR RICHARD PAID ROBIN HOOD

> *Grete well your abbot, sayd Robyn,*
> *And your pryour, I you pray,*
> *And byd hym send me such a monke,*
> *To dyner every day.*
> ANON: *A Lytell Geste of Robyn Hode* (1489)

SPRING came round again, and with it the day on which Sir Richard of Legh was to pay back to Robin Hood the four hundred pounds which had so narrowly saved his lands from the Abbot of St Mary's.

By living quietly at home and saving most of his rents, Sir Richard was able to set off at the appointed time not only with the four hundred pounds in his pouch, but accompanied by a troop of his own men who carried as presents for Robin a hundred good yew bows and as many sheaves of arrows with shining metal points and peacock feathers below the deep notches for the string.

As Sir Richard and his followers hastened along the road into Barnsdale they came to a bridge over the river where many of the people living nearby were met that day for a wrestling match. The prize was a white horse richly harnessed, a pair of gloves, a gold ring and a pipe of wine, and just as Sir Richard arrived, a tremendous uproar began round the ring where the wrestling was taking place.

Pushing through the crowd, he asked what was wrong and discovered that the favourite champion of the whole neighbourhood had just been thrown by an unknown yeoman who had appeared suddenly that day and entered for the wrestling.

'But is not the contest open to all comers?' asked Sir Richard.

'It is so, indeed,' answered the onlooker whom he was questioning, 'but the men of Barnsdale be jealous of an outsider like this Arthur-a-Bland, and I fear they will beat him and throw him into the river rather than let him carry off the prize.'

'This shame must not be!' exclaimed Sir Richard, and followed by his men he pushed his way to the centre of the crowd and struck up the cudgels which were raised to fell Arthur-a-Bland.

Sir Richard spoke to the gathering for some time, and the truth of his words, backed by the sight of his armed followers, brought them to their senses, and the prize was given to Arthur-a-Bland the true winner. Sir Richard then bought the wine from him for five marks and presented it to the crowd, who cheered him heartily and began to drink his health and the health of Arthur-a-Bland too as if they had never thought of cracking his skull or throwing him into the river.

But all this had taken some time, and hasten as he might, it was long past noon when Sir Richard came to the meeting place.

Meanwhile Robin and his men waited in vain for the coming of Sir Richard.

'Let us go to dinner,' said Little John at length.

'Not so,' answered Robin. 'I fear that Our Lady is wrath with me, since she has not sent me my pay!'

'Have no doubts, master!' cried Little John. 'It is scarcely noon. Be sure that before the sun is down, all will come right. I dare be sworn Sir Richard of Legh is true and trustworthy.'

'Then take your bows,' said Robin, 'you and Much

and Scarlet, and hasten to the Great North Road. And if the knight you cannot find, may be you will meet with another guest to stand proxy for him!'

Off went the three merry men, clad all in Lincoln green with swords at their sides and bows in their hands – but never a sign of Sir Richard could they find.

Presently, however, as they lay in wait behind the bushes, they saw two monks dressed in long black robes and riding on white palfreys, with a large band of serving men and attendants behind them.

Then said Little John to Much, with a broad grin: 'I'll wager my life these monks have brought our pay! So cheer up, loosen your swords in their scabbards, set arrows to your strings – and follow me. The monks have twenty or more followers I know – but I dare not return to Robin without his expected guests!'

So saying Little John sprang out into the road, followed by Much and Scarlet, levelled an arrow at the face of the leading monk, and exclaimed:

'Stay, churlish monk, and go no further! One more step, and you die! My arrow is aimed to strike an inch below your hat-band! So come along with me – my master is furious at being kept so long for his dinner.'

'Who is your master?' asked the monk, amazed by this sudden summons.

'Who else but bold Robin Hood!' answered Little John.

'He is a strong thief!' quavered the monk, pale with fear. 'I have heard little good of him!'

'You lie!' cried Little John, 'and you shall rue it! He is a good yeoman of the forest, and he bids you to dinner with him.'

'What if we refuse?' asked the monk.

'Then I loose mine arrow,' replied Little John calmly.

**When Little John made as though to raise his hand,
they fled with one accord**

'But my men will cut you down, all three of you!' hesitated the monk.

'I have a hundred bowmen hidden in the bushes on either side of the road,' declared Little John unblushingly. 'I have but to raise my hand, or cry an order, and every man here lies dead with an arrow in his heart!'

When they heard this, there was panic amongst the followers and attendants: and when Little John made as though to raise his hand, they turned with one accord and fled for their lives, leaving the two monks on their horses too petrified to move.

'We are well rid of them,' laughed Little John, 'since there are but three of us. Now then, you Much, and you Scarlet, lead our guests' horses by their bridles while I walk behind with an arrow on the string – in case of accidents.'

So they brought the two monks into Barnsdale where Robin was waiting for them, and Robin greeted them courteously.

'These are churlish guests,' protested Little John, 'and their followers were but cowards! Forty of them at least there were – and all ran away when they saw me bend my bow!'

'Well, summon our men to dinner,' laughed Robin, 'and let us make our guests as welcome as we can.'

'This is an outrage!' protested the first monk. 'I am the Abbot of St Mary's High Cellarer, and this reverent monk is my clerk.'

'High Cellarer, ha-ha!' said Robin. 'Then your duty is to supply the Abbey with provisions and wine – and also to collect tithes, both in kind and money. Maybe Our Lady has sent me my pay after all – by the hands of this her servant. . . . But to dinner first. Little John, fill a horn of the best wine for Master Cellarer – who doubtless is an expert on vintages – and let him drink to me!'

With a very bad grace the Cellarer and his Clerk drank the wine and made some pretence at eating.

'Well now,' said Robin presently. 'If you have indeed brought me my money, Master Cellarer, I pray you let me see it. And if you are ever in need, maybe I can do as much for you.'

'I know nothing of any moneys owing to you!' cried the Cellarer anxiously, 'and I have no money with me.'

'None at all?' queried Robin.

'But twenty shillings,' declared the Cellarer, 'I swear it before God. Twenty shillings for my journey, and no more.'

'Alas, poor man,' said Robin sympathetically. 'If that is indeed all you have, I'll give you as much again to help you on your way. . . . Little John, search the saddle-bags of these reverent gentlemen – and search them also, in case they may have forgotten an odd shilling or two.'

The Cellarer grew pale with fear, and his Clerk began to blubber and mutter prayers, while Little John spread a cloak on the ground and after a little search began heaping piles of shining gold and silver on it.

'Eight hundred pounds!' he declared at length. 'That is of gold alone. And yonder heap of silver will come to quite a few pounds over that sum.'

'Then Our Lady has sent me the money which I had lent to pay the Abbot,' said Robin. 'And by the Mass, she pays good interest! Fill up Master Cellarer's cup, and his Clerk's cup also. But tell me, sirs, whither were you going?'

'To seek his Royal Highness, Prince John,' answered the Cellarer. 'The money was for him – and cruel indeed will be the interest he will extort from you if you

dare to touch a penny of it! I took with me also a message from the Lord Abbot about taking steps to humble
the treasonable pride of a certain Sir Richard of Legh
who is a law-breaker that defies Holy Church in the
person of the said Abbot.'

'The said knight,' quoth Robin, mimicking the pom-
pous tones of the frightened Cellarer, 'is a good friend
to me – and the said Prince John a traitor to his brother
our good King Richard. . . . The gold was intended for
the royal coffers, was it, Master Cellarer?'

'Yes, indeed it was!'

'Then we will keep it for King Richard. And as for
the silver, that we will keep in payment for the good
food and wine our guests have partaken of while with us.'

'Alas that ever we came into this place!' lamented the
Cellarer. 'How much cheaper our dinner would have
been in Blythe or Doncaster!'

'Go now back to York,' said Robin sternly. 'Greet
your Abbot from me: tell him to beware how he
oppresses Sir Richard of Legh any further – and bid him
send me such a guest as yourself to dinner every day!'

Scarcely had the Cellarer and his Clerk ridden away,
lamenting the loss of their money and threatening dire
revenges on Robin Hood and his men, when Sir Richard
of Legh came riding hastily to the meeting place with
his little troop behind him.

'Greetings to you, good sir knight!' cried Robin gaily.
'But what brings you here into Barnsdale? No ill, I
hope? Surely the Abbot of St Mary's has not taken your
house and lands from you in spite of all?'

'By God's good grace and your kindness,' answered
Sir Richard gravely, 'my house and lands are mine once
more, free from all debt, mortgage or other incum-
brance. But I pray you forgive me that I am late at the

tryst: on the way I came upon a wrestling, where a good yeoman called Arthur-a-Bland was like to have suffered wrong and ill usage had I not stopped to help him.'

'Forgive!' cried Robin. 'Rather I thank you from my heart for what you did – any man who stays to help a good yeoman earns my friendship for ever.'

'I thank you,' said Sir Richard. 'But now take this money which I owe you, the four hundred pounds that saved my estate. And with it this twenty pounds more by way of interest.'

'But, my good friend,' said Robin very seriously. 'You owe me no money. It has already been paid: Our Lady, by the hands of the Cellarer of St Mary's, paid the full four hundred pounds scarce an hour since – and a good four hundred more by way of interest. And if I took it twice, I were shamed for ever. But truly, gentle knight, you yourself are more welcome than any money could be.'

Sir Richard hardly knew what to say or think at this, but Robin Hood soon told him of what had happened, and they laughed together heartily over it.

'But on my honour,' said Sir Richard at length, 'here *is* the money I owe you.'

'Use it well,' answered Robin, 'buy a good horse and good armour in case you have need to fight for our noble King Richard, or to defend any other good yeoman. . . . Or to defend yourself; I fear much lest the Abbot or Prince John accuse you of being in league with me in this matter of lightening Master Cellarer's purse – and do you some ill deed.'

'You certainly stand in great danger,' answered Sir Richard, 'and both the Abbot and the Sheriff will be out after you for this. Therefore accept these small gifts I have brought with me for you: a hundred good yew bows, cut and seasoned on my estate at Legh, and a hundred sheaves of arrows, true and straight and well feathered.'

'I accept them gladly,' said Robin. 'As you say, we may need them soon. . . . But come now, noon is not so long past but that a good stoop of wine would come amiss. And tonight we will feast you right royally. . . .'

CHAPTER TEN

THE SILVER ARROW

I'll send this arrow from my bow,
And in a wager will be bound
To hit the mark aright, although
It were for fifteen hundred pound.
Doubt not I'll make the wager good,
Or ne'er believe bold Robin Hood.

ANON: *Robin Hood's Garland (c. 1723)*

SIR RICHARD OF LEGH was right when he warned Robin Hood that the Abbot of St Mary's was not a man to forgive or forget such injuries and disappointments as he had suffered. But there was no sign of any warlike expedition either against Robin in Sherwood or against Sir Richard in his Cheshire home.

News came to Robin, however, not so very long after that Prince John, who was at that time travelling about the country with a large court of his especial followers, was holding a great archery contest in Cheshire. He was doing this, so rumour said, because a dispute had arisen between the Foresters of the Forests of Delamere and Wirral as to which were the best archers: and Prince John – hoping to increase his popularity – had proclaimed this great archery meeting, and thrown the contest open to the archers of the other northern forests such as Barnsdale, Plompton, and Sherwood. Furthermore, it was said that the prize which would be given to the best archer was an arrow made all of silver, with head and feathers of rich red gold.

'I think,' said Robin, when he heard all this, 'that we

should show Prince John that a Sherwood archer can shoot as well or better than any Delamere man. .... As for that silver arrow, I have a great desire to drop it into my quiver!'

'We shall be in great danger,' said Scarlet cautiously. 'Prince John will certainly remember the outlawed Earl of Huntingdon – even if his servant has slipped his memory.'

Little John nodded. 'And maybe,' he said, 'our enemies in Nottingham and York will expect Robin to compete for this arrow – and be ready for him should he dare to show himself at this shooting match.'

Robin Hood smiled slowly. 'Exactly,' he said, 'should I *show* myself. But can I not go in disguise? Just I myself, since this is really rather a fool's errand, and it is not right that I should risk any lives but my own.'

'Never will I hear of it!' exclaimed Little John indignantly.

'Nor I!' echoed Scarlet. 'If you go, we go also – and the pick of our good fellows lie in wait near the butts in case of accident. . . .'

The match was held on a bright October day, under a cold sun, with a touch of frost in the air to bring vigour and alertness to all who stood forth to show their prowess with the long-bow and cloth-yard shaft.

At Kingslea Park, on the edge of Delamere Forest, near the home of Sir Richard de Kingsley, Hereditary High Forester of Wirral and Delamere, a gay concourse was gathered together. Prince John, surrounded by the Knights and Gentlemen of Cheshire, and a fair number of his own followers, sat on a raised stand near the targets, and a large gathering of yeomen, foresters, and many others lined either side of the long strip of greensward which divided the archers from their targets.

All through the day the competitors shot and shot, with many a pause for refreshment. Prince John, to increase his popularity among the poorer sort, was giving free beef and beer to all comers that day – and found it hard to smile as more and more came trooping in from every direction to enjoy the shooting and his hospitality.

When the afternoon was far advanced all the heats had been shot off, leaving only six archers to compete – one from each of the forests. The excitement grew intense as each of them took their stand on the line and in turn sent the twenty-eight inch arrows singing down the glade to the great target nearly a quarter of a mile away.

Up near the butts the excitement grew into wild enthusiasm as one by one the arrows came whizzing into the target with a sharp zip of tearing canvas. The long-drawn call 'He! He!' from each archer came ringing up the course, and in the hush that followed his arrow whistled through the air like a brown gleam of light.

Three arrows struck in the gold, two in the red which came next to it, and one in the black ring which was beyond the blue but better than the outside white. Yells of joy and triumph rose when it was proclaimed that both Delamere and Wirral were in the gold – the third arrow representing Sherwood.

'And now,' said Sir Richard de Kingsley, 'since these three are equal, let them shoot at the eye – and that be the final test.'

So saying, he went down himself to the target and marked a little white eye in the centre of the great gold disc which shone in the light of the afternoon sun. When this was done, he returned to his place beside Prince John and blew a call on his bugle to bid the archers begin.

Then first the man from Delamere stood forward, gave his long, low cry of 'He! He!', notched his arrow,

drew it to his cheek until the point was scarce an inch
from the hand which gripped the bow – and loosed. The
arrow hummed through the air, and a long sigh from
the crowd went with it. Sir Richard stepped down to the
target.

'In the gold!' he cried. 'But a hair's breadth out from
the eye!'

In breathless silence the man from Wirral set the
notch to the string, drew, hung a moment on the aim,
and loosed – a tense murmur flying with the arrow and
rising into excitement as it struck into the canvas.

'Then Wirral has it!' declared Sir Richard. 'Unless
Sherwood shoot better. The arrow is on the very line,
and the white of the eye is wounded by it.'

Once more his bugle rang out, and every sound died
with the echo of it. Quietly the man from Sherwood
took his stand, notched the arrow, drew the string,
glanced down the point at the distant target, and loosed
with a calm air of certainty, striding up the course
before ever it had reached the target.

As the arrow went on its way all heads turned to
follow its course as if a great wind went with it, and the
sound of its flight was drowned by a long moan which
followed it, a moan of indrawn breaths which burst out
with a cry of mingled praise and disappointment as Sir
Richard de Kingsley proclaimed in a great voice:

'True to the centre of the eye! I declare that Sherwood bears away the silver arrow from both Wirral and
Delamere! Let the champion, the man of Sherwood,
draw near and receive his prize.'

With his hood still over his head, the tall archer
mounted the steps and knelt before Prince John.

'Uncover, fellow, uncover!' gasped the Sheriff of
Chester in scandalized tones, and leaning forward he
himself pulled back the archer's hood.

The sound of the flight was drowned by the
long moan which followed it

'I herewith bestow this silver arrow upon the best archer present,' proclaimed Prince John, 'and declare that, by the proof shown today, the archers of Sherwood outdo all others in skill, the archers of Wirral being second – a hair's breadth ahead of the archers of Delamere.'

'I thank your Royal Highness,' answered the archer of Sherwood, inclining his head as he took the arrow.

'What is your name, good yeoman?' asked Prince John.

'Robert Fitzwilliam,' was the answer.

A knight dressed in chain mail, sitting behind Prince John, leant forward suddenly, scanned the speaker's face, and then said quietly:

'Once known as Fitzooth, and falsely called Earl of Huntingdon?'

'Yes, Sir Guy of Gisborne,' came the answer. 'Once known as Fitzooth, and truly the Earl of Huntingdon.'

'And now a traitor and an outlaw,' added Prince John, his lips curling in a wolfish snarl. 'Well, I am glad to have seen this far-famed Robin Hood – before I see him gracing a gallows.'

'Shame upon you, false Prince!' cried Robin, drawing himself up to his full height. 'This is no way to treat a guest, and the lawful winner of your prize.'

Prince John was about to answer, when Sir Guy leaned over his shoulder and whispered something to him.

'Go in peace this once, false traitor,' said John, 'but we shall meet again!'

With that Robin bowed, eyed Sir Guy coldly for a moment, and descended from the stand. The moment he was gone Sir Guy was away behind the stand, while Prince John remarked to the Sheriff of Chester:

'To take him here might have caused a riot – and

undone all today's good work. But Sir Guy has men posted on every road, and he cannot escape. A clever trap indeed: Sir Guy knew his man well when he said that it was a bait this fellow could never resist!'

'We are in great danger,' said Robin in a low voice to Little John and Scarlet who were waiting for him in the crowd. 'Gather the rest of our band and slip quietly away to the northwards where Delamere Forest lies deepest. If they overtake us, fire a volley, and then flee into the Forest: it will be dark in a couple of hours. If we lose one another, let each make his way separately to the trysting place in Sherwood.'

The danger came upon them sooner than Robin had expected. They were not yet out of Kingslea Park when the bushes on every side gave up armed men, and a shrill bugle call brought Sir Guy with several mounted followers galloping across the open towards them.

'Now stand all together,' directed Robin, 'and shoot as you never shot before. Not one volley, but many, keeping back three or four arrows each man. There are but a dozen of us and at least four times that number of them – but has not today shown that the archers of Sherwood surpass all others?'

'Yield, Robin Hood!' shouted Sir Guy as soon as he was near enough. 'My men surround you, and there is no escape!'

'That rests with God,' answered Robin. 'And *this* is my answer to you, Sir Guy!' As he spoke Robin drew his bow, loosed, the arrow hummed from the string and struck Guy of Gisborne on the front of his helmet. It failed to pierce the iron plate, but it toppled him backwards out of his saddle, and brought him to the ground with a crash.

Then the air grew dark with arrows, the men of

Sherwood aiming and loosing with an almost incredible speed and accuracy, bringing down man after man of Sir Guy's party dead or wounded. Two of Robin's men fell dead beneath the answering arrows, but in a little while no one durst stand against the archers of Sherwood but fled in all directions pursued by the grim brown arrows.

'Now,' commanded Robin, 'shoot no more but turn and run for the trees before they come again with reinforcements.'

But they were not to get away so easily. Sir Guy had recovered his senses and was up on horse-back again, urging on his men, while parties kept running in from various glades and rides in the Forest, which was almost continuously open in that part.

Twice small bands of men sprang on them out of ambush, and were only beaten back with quick volleys of arrows, and three more of Robin's men had fallen by the time the darkness began to gather.

They were speeding along a wide, open glade now, and here the greatest disaster of all befell them. A small party of Sir Guy's men came suddenly out of a side path ahead of them and discharged a valley of arrows. The answering volley sent them scurrying back among the trees, but the harm was done: Little John was hurt full sore with an arrow in his knee, so that he could run no longer, nor even stand upon that leg.

'Good Master,' then said Little John to Robin, 'for the love of God, and for my love to you, and for all the service I have done you, never let Sir Guy find me alive and hang me. I can run no longer, and it were death to us all did you stay to defend me: therefore I pray you draw your good sword and smite off my head, or strike me to the heart, so that no life may be left in me when Sir Guy comes.'

'Dear John, for all the gold in merry England I would not have you dead and myself still living,' answered Robin. 'No, though it leave Marian a widow ere she be wed, I would rather die at your side.'

'God forbid that we should ever leave you behind us,' echoed Scarlet.

'Help him on to my back,' commanded Robin curtly. 'The rest of you follow behind, and shoot – but only when you can be certain of hitting your mark. Our arrows are nearly spent. Much, you are the youngest and nimblest – run on ahead and see if you can find any place of reasonable safety. Once darkness falls, we shall be safe enough – but only if we have got unseen into our hiding-place.'

They had proceeded but a little way, when Much came running back to them.

'Yonder is a fine stone house,' he exclaimed, 'with towers and a good moat of water!'

'If it be but the home of a friend!' gasped Robin. 'Much, did you note any crest or coat of arms, or other blazoning whereby we may tell who dwells there?'

'Yes indeed,' answered Much, 'on a great slab of stone over the doorway is a shield painted gold, with a great ramping lion in red upon it.'

'On a shield Or a Lion Rampant, Gules!' said Robin. 'Then our prayers are heard! Those are the arms of our good friend Sir Richard of Legh. Run back quickly, Much, sound our call upon your horn, and beg shelter for us of Sir Richard.'

Much did as he was told, and when Robin and his men came to the moat side, the bridge was down and Sir Richard himself there to greet them.

'Welcome, welcome are you to me, bold Robin Hood!' he cried. 'I am overjoyed that so speedily the chance is given to me of repaying your great kindness shown to me when I was with you in Barnsdale.'

'I bring you great danger!' gasped Robin, setting down Little John in the entrance way. 'Sir Guy of Gisborne follows with many men, and Prince John, now at Kingslea, will not let you shield me without striving to punish you.'

'Come all within my hall,' said Sir Richard, and when they were in, he bade his men draw up the bridge and defend the walls and the great tower. 'I owe no allegiance to Prince John,' he continued grimly. 'Under King Richard, Ranulph Earl of Chester is my only over-lord – and so this upstart knight of Gisborne shall learn to his cost! But as for you, friend Robin, and for these your men, I shall hold you prisoners here for twelve days at least – and entertain you as royally as I may!'

Early next morning came Sir Guy of Gisborne with a large company of men, and demanded that Sir Richard of Legh should surrender Robin Hood and the other outlaws of Sherwood to him.

Sir Richard answered him courteously but firmly.

'I am lord paramount of Legh,' he said, 'and only my over-lord, the Earl of Chester, has the right you seek – and of course the King himself. Robert of Locksley is my guest: I know nothing of this outlawry – which may hold good in Nottingham, but has no royal sanction in Cheshire. You, Sir Guy, a knight and a gentleman of coat armour, know well that neither by the laws of chivalry nor of hospitality can I surrender any guest within my gates to any but Royal authority.'

After this Sir Guy went away, and when the twelve days were up, Robin and his men bade farewell to kind Sir Richard and set out for Sherwood, Little John riding on horseback since his knee was not yet fully recovered.

But Robin was right in warning Sir Richard that Prince John would not let him rest in peace after crossing his will. Sir Guy had not dared to attack the house of Legh without fuller authority, and by the time he had overtaken Prince John (who was already on his way back to London) and could return with his mandate Robin and his party were back in Sherwood. Sir Guy did not then think it worth while to attack the heavily fortified house, but he and a picked band waited in the neighbourhood until one day Sir Richard, thinking no danger, went out hawking with only two attendants. Then they fell upon him from an ambush, took him captive and hustled him away to Nottingham where they cast him into prison.

Then Sir Richard's lady mounted her horse and with two followers only rode day and night until she came to Sherwood.

'God save you, Robin Hood!' she cried when she had been found by several of his men and led to the secret glade. 'For the love of Our Lady use all the power you have! Sir Guy of Gisborne has taken my husband, contrary to all law, and it is said that he is imprisoned in Nottingham Castle.'

'We can scarce effect a rescue there,' said Robin, looking grave. 'But I will come with you this instant and we will together to Chester there to beg the aid of Earl Ranulph – who will not lightly allow his liegeman to suffer durance in any shire but his own.'

Robin did as he promised, and it is a matter of history how Ranulph, Earl of Chester – as much a king in his own County Palatine as ever a king was of England in those days – defied Prince John and marched a small army of Cheshire men against Nottingham.

And the outcome was that Sir Richard of Legh was

released from prison and escorted with all honour back to his own home – where neither Sir Guy of Gisborne nor John himself, even after he became King, ever dared to molest him again, however often he might entertain Robin Hood or any of his merry men.

CHAPTER ELEVEN

ROBIN HOOD AND THE BUTCHER

And thou, fine fellowe, who has tasted so
Of the forester's greenwood game,
Will be in no haste thy time to waste
In seeking more taste of the same:
Of this can I read thee and riddle thee well,
Thou hast better by far be the devil in hell,
Than the Sheriff of Nottingham!

THOMAS LOVE PEACOCK: *Maid Marian (1822)*

ALTHOUGH there was so much to do in Sherwood where nearly all of the food they ate had to be hunted, trapped, or shot, and they were always in danger of surprise from the Sheriff of Nottingham, Sir Guy of Gisborne, and the rest, Robin Hood occasionally found time hang heavy on his hands.

On one such occasion he and Little John were walking by the high road to Nottingham where it runs through the forest, when they saw a Butcher with his cart of meat come jogging along on his way to market.

'Yonder comes a proud fellow,' said Little John, 'who fancies himself a master with the quarter staff. He comes through the forest twice every week, and nothing gives him greater pleasure than the chance to thrash someone with his big stick.'

'Twice a week,' said Robin, 'and he has never paid any toll to us! It is long since I fought with the quarter staff, except in friendly wise with you or Friar Tuck. I'll go and have words with this Butcher – and see if blows come of it!'

'I'll wager a piece of gold he beats you!' said Little
John.

'Done!' smiled Robin, and laying aside his weapons,
he cut himself a good oak staff and strode down the road
until he met the Butcher.

'Now then!' cried the Butcher sharply, as Robin laid
a hand on the horse's bridle. 'What do you want, you
impudent fellow?'

'You have haunted these ways long enough,' said
Robin sternly, 'without paying the due toll that you
owe to me! Come, sirrah, pay up at once!'

'And who do you think you are?' cried the Butcher.
'A Forest Guard or what? I serve the good Sheriff of
Nottingham – and he'll make your hide smart for this,
after I've tanned you myself, and broken your head into
the bargain.'

'I am of Robin Hood's company,' was the reply, 'and
if you will not pay tribute in gold, get down out of that
cart and pay it in blows.'

'Right willingly!' answered the Butcher, and jumping out of his cart he charged at Robin, whirling his
staff about his head.

Then there was as good a fight, and as pretty a play of
skill with the quarter staves as ever one might see: but
the long and short of it was that though Robin suffered
a sore clout over one eye, in the end he brought the
Butcher to the ground with a last stunning blow.

'The piece of gold is yours,' said Little John coming
up.

'This is a fine fellow,' said Robin as the Butcher sat
up and looked about him. 'Give him wine, Little John,
I'll warrant his head is ringing even louder than mine!'

'That it is!' groaned the Butcher. 'By the Mass, you
are a bonny fighter. I think you must be Robin Hood
himself, and no other!'

'That I am indeed!' said Robin.

'Then I think no shame at being beaten,' said the Butcher with a sigh of relief. 'And I'll willingly pay any toll you may ask of me.'

'No, no,' answered Robin, 'you've paid toll enough with that broken head of yours. Come now to our camp and see what good cheer we can make for you.'

When the meal was over, Robin said suddenly to the Butcher:

'Good friend, I have a mind to be a butcher myself. Will you sell me your horse, your cart and the meat now on it for ten pounds – and stay here in the forest with us?'

'Right willingly,' answered the Butcher, and the deal was made.

'You go into danger for no good cause,' said Will Scarlet doubtfully as Robin donned the Butcher's garb.

'Nevertheless I go,' answered Robin. 'I grow weary of this unchanging forest life – and also I would have news of what passes in the world outside. It is said that King Richard is a prisoner somewhere in Europe, and Prince John makes no effort to find and ransom him: I would know more of this. Never fear, not even the Sheriff will know me!'

With that Robin fixed a black patch over one eye, climbed into the cart and went rattling away through the forest and onto the Nottingham road once more. In the afternoon he came to Nottingham, drew up his cart in the market-place, and began to cry:

'Meat to sell! Fresh meat to sell! Fresh meat a penny a pound!'

Then all that saw and heard him at his trade said that he had not been a Butcher for long, since at that price he could not expect to earn a living. But the thrifty housewives gathered round him eagerly, for never had they bought such cheap meat before.

Among them came the Sheriff's wife, and seeing that
the meat was good, fresh and tender – and most un-
usually cheap, she invited the Butcher to bring his cart
up to the Sheriff's house, sell to her what was left, and
then sup with her and the Sheriff.

Robin accepted with delight, and as evening fell he
stabled his horse and empty cart in the Sheriff's stables
and sat down to dine as an honoured guest at the
Sheriff's board.

All said he had not been a butcher for long!

At dinner that night Robin learned many things
which he wished to know. He heard that King Richard
was in truth a prisoner, but that Prince John was giving
out that he was dead so that he himself might become
King.

'But a pestilent fellow called Blondel,' added the
Sheriff, 'has gone in search of Richard. He is a minstrel,

and so can pass unmolested through the most hostile
lands: may the plague take him speedily!'

'Will the great Barons and the Lords and Knights
accept Prince John as King?' asked Robin.

'There the trouble lies,' said the Sheriff shaking his
head sadly. 'Many, like the Earl of Chester, oppose him.
But many more will be won over . . .'

Later in the evening the Sheriff asked Robin if he had
any horned beasts that he could sell to him – meaning
live cattle rather than joints of meat.

'Yes, that I have, good master Sheriff,' answered
Robin, 'I have two or three hundred of them, and many
an acre of good free land, if you please to see it. I can let it
to you with as good a right as ever my father made to me.'

'The horned beasts interest me most,' said the Sheriff.
'Good master Butcher, I will come with you on the
morrow – and make you a right fair offer for the whole
herd, if they please me.'

Robin Hood slept well and comfortably in the
Sheriff's house, and ate a fine breakfast in the morning
before they set off together, accompanied by only two
men, to see the horned beasts.

The Sheriff seemed in high spirits when they started
out, jesting and laughing with Robin. But presently as
they went deeper and deeper into Sherwood Forest he
grew more and more silent.

'Have we much further to go, friend Butcher?' he
asked at last. 'God protect us this day from a man they
call Robin Hood!'

'The outlaw, you mean?' asked Robin. 'I know him
well, and have often shot at the butts with him. I am no
bad archer myself, if it comes to that: indeed I dare
swear that Robin Hood himself can shoot no better
than I.'

'Know you where he lies hid in Sherwood?' asked the
Sheriff eagerly.

'Right well,' replied Robin, 'even his most secret
place of hiding.'

'I would pay you well if you were to bring me
thither,' said the Sheriff.

'That will I do,' answered Robin. 'But hist now: we
draw near the place where the horned beasts are to be
found. Stay a moment, while I wind my horn so that the
herdsmen may drive them hither.'

So saying Robin set his horn to his mouth and blew
three blasts. Then he drew a little behind the Sheriff and
waited.

Presently there was a crackling in the thicket, and a
great troop of red deer came into view, tossing their
antlers proudly.

'How like you my horned beasts, Master Sheriff?'
asked Robin. 'They be fat and fair to see!'

'Good fellow, I wish I were far from here,' said the
Sheriff uncomfortably. 'I like not your company . . .'

'We will have better company anon,' Robin remarked with a smile, and even as he spoke out of the
thicket came Little John, followed by Will Scarlet,
Much, Reynolde, William of Goldsbrough, and many
another of the outlaws of Sherwood.

'What is your will, good master?' said Little John.
'Come, tell us how you fared in Nottingham, and
whether you did good trade as a butcher?'

'Fine trade indeed,' answered Robin, pulling off his
eye-patch and the rest of his disguise. 'And see, I have
brought with me the Sheriff of Nottingham to dine with
us this day.'

'He is right welcome,' said Little John. 'And I am
sure he will pay well for his dinner.'

'Well indeed,' laughed Robin. 'For he has brought

much money with him to buy three hundred head of deer from me. And even now he offered me a great sum to lead him to our secret glade.'

'By the Rood,' said the Sheriff, shaking with terror, 'had I guessed who you were, a thousand pounds would not have brought me into Sherwood!'

'I would that you had a thousand pounds to bring you *out* of Sherwood,' said Robin. 'Now then, bind him and his men, blindfold them, and lead them to dinner. When we reach the glade we can see what they have brought us – and by then I will have earned every penny, ha, ha!'

So the Sheriff and his two trembling followers were blindfolded and led by the secret paths to the hidden glen, and Robin feasted them there full well. But afterwards he bade Little John spread his cloak upon the ground and pour into it all the money the Sheriff had brought with him, and the sum came to nearly five hundred pounds.

'We will keep the three good horses also,' said Robin, 'and let Master Sheriff and his two men walk back to Nottingham – for the good of their health. But let Maid Marian send a present of needlework to the Sheriff's lady, for she entertained me well at dinner and set fair dishes before me.'

Then the Sheriff and his two men were blindfolded once more and taken back to the Nottingham road, and there Robin bade them farewell.

'You shall not defy me for much longer, Robin Hood,' cried the Sheriff, shaking his fist at Robin in farewell. 'I'll come against you with a great force, depend upon it, and hang every man of you from the trees by this road side. And your head shall rot over Nottingham gate.'

'When next you come to visit me in Sherwood,' said

Robin quietly, 'you shall not get away on such easy terms. Come when you will, and the more of you the merrier – and I'll send you all packing back to Nottingham in your shirts!'

Then he left them and returned to the secret glade where the Butcher, whose name was Gilbert-of-the-White-Hand, was waiting for him.

'Here are your cart and horses back again, good master Butcher,' said Robin. 'I have had a fine holiday selling meat in your stead – but we must not play too many of such pranks.'

'By the Mass,' swore Gilbert the Butcher, 'I'll sell meat no longer, if you will have me as one of your merry men here in the greenwood. I cannot shoot with any skill – for see how my left hand was burnt white with fire when I once shot a deer to feed my starving family. But you have had some little proof of how I can smite with the quarter-staff.'

'Proof enough, good Gilbert,' cried Robin. 'I am right glad to welcome you as one of us. . . . Come, Friar Tuck, propound the oath to him. And then to dinner, and we'll all drink to the health of our new companion, Gilbert-of-the-White-Hand, the jolly Butcher of Nottingham!'

CHAPTER TWELVE

THE ADVENTURE OF THE BEGGARS

> *Our hearts they are stout and our bows they are good*
> *As well their masters know;*
> *They're cull'd in the forest of merry Sherwood,*
> *And never will spare a foe.*
>
> **MOSES MENDEZ:** *Robin Hood: An Opera* (*1751*)

AFTER Robin's adventure with the Butcher, Gilbert-of-the-White-Hand, and his trick played on the Sheriff of Nottingham, Little John professed himself to be jealous.

'I must change clothes with some body,' he said, 'and go into Nottingham, and beard master Sheriff! Robin Hood must not be the only man who has dared do it!'

Robin laughed: 'I would scarcely risk it again without good cause: one does not put one's head into a lion's mouth twice over. I escaped scathless – but you may not.'

Little John, however, was determined, and one day when he and Robin were walking through the Forest together, the chance came to him.

There were in those days a great many beggars wandering about the country – and they were not always either too old or too maimed to work: often indeed they were lazy ruffians who, if they could not get what they wanted by begging, turned as readily to force or even murder.

Such a beggar as this Robin and John saw striding along the road waving a great staff in his hand and singing merrily. He was strangely dressed in ragged clothes but so many folds of these that they would have kept out any weather; his hat was of the same kind – three old hats stuffed into each other and stuck together – and round his neck hung a great leather bag.

'There's your man!' said Robin. 'Go and change clothes with him, Little John – and I'll warrant the Sheriff will never know you.'

'The very thought had already come to me,' said Little John. 'Stay you here, good master, and see the sport.'

So Little John ran down onto the road and stood in front of the beggar.

'Tarry, tarry!' cried he. 'Indeed you must tarry!'

'Not I,' answered the beggar. 'It grows late, it's far to my lodging, and I'll look a fool if I get there to find all the supper finished.'

'Ah,' said Little John, 'I see that you think only of your own supper. But what about me? I have gone without a meal all this day: will you not help me to my supper ere you hasten to yours?'

'A likely thing indeed,' scoffed the beggar. 'I have no more than the one penny which will purchase mine.'

'Then give me that!' cried Little John.

'By the Mass,' answered the beggar, 'I'll give you more than that! I'll give you the biggest thrashing you ever had in your life!'

With that he threw off his cloak and bag, and made for Little John with his quarter-staff lifted. So they fought, striking each other many shrewd blows, while Robin sat hidden on the hillside and watched.

Presently he saw the beggar knock Little John to the ground, and he hastily fitted an arrow to his bow and waited to see what would happen.

'Ha, ha, my fine fellow!' jeered the beggar. 'You'd take the last penny from a poor man, would you? I'll show you what it's like to be a beggar!'

With that he stripped off Little John's fine doublet, hose, hood, and cloak, and put them on in place of his own ragged gown and three-piece hat, took up his bag once more, put Little John's purse into it, and set off up the road laughing to himself, while Little John sat up slowly and looked ruefully after him.

'Farewell, beggar John!' laughed Robin as he came down the hill. 'There you have your disguise; hie away to Nottingham and call on the Sheriff!'

'By the Rood!' said Little John, rubbing his head, 'I seem to have lost the first round. But I'll wager you, good master, that I'll bring back better gains as a beggar than ever you would!'

'Done!' laughed Robin. 'Now I'll hasten after your friend there and see what he has in his bag.'

Away went Robin at his best pace, and very soon caught up with the beggar. 'Not so fast, there!' shouted Robin. 'Stand still a minute while I come and break your head as you have broken my companion's!'

'I'm always ready to give alms of that sort,' answered the beggar cheerfully. 'And when I've thrashed you, I'll have a change of fine clothes – just like any squire in the country!'

To it they went with their staves, but this time it was the beggar who went down while Robin stood victorious over him, drawing his hunting-knife as he did so.

'Ah, spare me!' cried the beggar, 'be good to me! What will you gain by butchering so poor a wretch as I? I fought in my own defence – and only punished your friend as I thought proper for his presumption. . . . Look you, good sir, I have a hundred pounds hidden in my bag, and all that will I pay you for my life.'

'So,' said Robin, sheathing his knife. 'A beggar has more than a penny to bless himself with. Well, my fine fellow, let me see the colour of your gold.'

'Right willingly,' answered the beggar. And with that he opened the great bag and drew from it a cloak which he spread upon the ground. He put his hand into the bag again, and Robin bent down to see what he would take out, the brisk wind ruffling his hair as he did so. The beggar moved round a little so as to get the wind behind him. And then he suddenly pulled out a great handful of finely ground meal and flung it into Robin's face.

Robin was quite blinded for the moment and could do nothing but cough and rub his eyes; and while he did so the beggar snatched up his staff and laid him out with a good blow on the back of his head. Then he stripped off Robin's cloak, hood and doublet, took his purse also, crammed them into his bag, and set off again, laughing heartily at his own cleverness.

Little John, now dressed as a beggar, came along the road just as Robin sat up and looked about him.

'We're equal now, good master,' he said with a grin. 'Yonder beggar has left you his second coat – and you have your hose. . . . Now I'm off to see what I can win back from this fellow.'

'The day is not over yet,' gasped Robin. 'I may still bring the biggest booty to the trysting tree!'

He got slowly to his feet after Little John had left him, and put on the beggar's second coat – which happened to be a better one than the strange, ragged garment which Little John was wearing. Then he went back to the hillside where he had left his bow, his quiver of arrows – and his horn.

Robin stowed away the arrows under his coat, unstrung the bow which he could then use as a staff, and set off by the shortest forest paths towards Nottingham.

He was well enough disguised, for his hair and beard were now all matted and tangled with blood and caked meal, and he had one black eye.

Through the wood he went, and at length he came to the edge of the forest where a great open meadow sloped down to the walls of Nottingham. Here he found a large gathering of people who had evidently flocked out from the city to see a hanging, for the place round which they were clustered was a low knoll on which stood the gallows.

'This is no public spectacle, but cruel, unlawful wickedness,' said Robin

Robin shouldered his way into the crowd and soon came near the front, where he paused to ask what was going on. He was told that three young men had been caught killing deer in Sherwood, and as Prince John had left special instructions on his last visit to Nottingham that the Forest Laws were to be strictly enforced, all three of them were to be blinded with hot irons.

'This is no public spectacle, but a cruel, unlawful wickedness,' said Robin.

'Aye, so it is, good beggar,' agreed a stout yeoman who stood beside him. 'But the Sheriff has proclaimed that this horror must be done in public – as a warning to other people.'

'Are you free Englishmen and will raise no hand to save these poor youths?' asked Robin.

'There are twenty of the Sheriff's guard, armed with swords,' answered the yeoman sullenly. 'Moreover most of us are known men – and if we raised a hand not only we, but our wives and children would suffer. . . . And the youths *have* broken the law.'

Robin pushed his way right to the front. The crowd was crying shame upon the Sheriff, Prince John, and all Normans – and pity and encouragement to the prisoners. Robin shouted louder than anyone else, but his words were of hatred to the three law breakers.

Presently a man in a leather apron, obviously the executioner, strode past, and drew a wicked-looking iron shaped like a tuning fork from a brazier, and after deciding that it was hot enough, started back again towards the prisoners.

But by now the crowd had closed up even nearer. The executioner had almost to push his way. As he passed Robin, he tripped suddenly. Robin uttered a cry, lurched forward as if pushed from behind, and landed on the man's back.

There was an awful yell, and the crowd drew away hastily as the captain of the guard strode forward with several of his men. Roughly they dragged Robin to his feet, and then the executioner. But the latter fell again, and writhed upon the ground – for the hot iron in his hand had burned a great red wound like the letter U on his face – and in falling Robin had broken several of his ribs.

'Your noble worships!' whined Robin. 'The crowd pushed me – I fell – I could not help it. Oh, do not punish a poor beggar! Spare me, I pray!'

'Hold him down and give him twenty strokes with a belt!' ordered the Captain. 'Or stay. Fellow, you may go free if you perform the office of executioner in place of the man whom you have injured.'

'Right willingly, oh right willingly, most noble sir!' exclaimed Robin, while the crowd groaned, and then cursed him.

'Make haste then,' said the captain. 'There will be trouble if we delay longer.'

'Let me first see that the villains are well bound,' said Robin, and picking up the bow which he was using as a staff, he limped towards the gallows to the base of which the three young men were lashed securely with thick ropes.

Robin examined each in turn, bending low over them and fingering the knots. Then, leaving his staff behind, he limped back to the brazier, picking up the iron as he went.

'As soon as this iron's white hot,' he called out, 'I'll see that the right man gets it in the face!'

The captain then stood forward and once more read out the charge against the three men, the law which they had broken, the punishment appointed, and Prince John's special charge as to its enforcement. Before he had finished Robin took the iron out of the fire and carried it all glowing hot towards the gallows, while a low murmur of hate and loathing rippled round the crowd.

Robin came to the foot of the gallows, raised the iron as if to press the points into the first man's eyes – and then he turned suddenly, straightened himself up and hurled it with deadly accuracy into the face of the captain of the guard.

There was a moment of petrified silence and stillness, broken only by the captain's yell of agony. During it Robin flung off the beggar's coat, took up his bow, and had an arrow ready on the string as he cried in a ringing voice:

'Freemen of England – make way for Robin Hood and his three new followers!'

'Cut him down!' cried the captain, staggering to his feet. Robin's bowstring twanged, and the captain fell to the ground for the last time, an arrow in his heart. And even, it seemed, as the string twanged, there was another arrow waiting upon it.

Meanwhile the three prisoners had slipped their bonds, which Robin had untied while making pretence to secure them, and one of them leapt forward and snatched the sword and shield from the dead captain.

Now the guards made as if to attack Robin. But his bowstring twanged twice, and two more men lay dead – for at that range even chain mail could not withstand arrows sped by the surest hand that ever plucked bowstring. They hesitated, and while they did, the three young men charged upon them where the line was thinnest, broke through, and in a moment were lost in the crowd. Robin loosed one more arrow, and then the crowd received him too, and although no force or defiance were used, the guards could only push through the throng slowly – while Robin and the men whom he had rescued passed out and away into Sherwood Forest as if the hillside had been empty.

While all this was happening by Nottingham, Little John, dressed as a beggar and thirsting for revenge, was hastening through the forest paths in search of his late adversary.

He came up with him late in the afternoon in a little forest glade just off the high road. Here a fire had been lit, and round it sat three other beggars besides the man he was after – and one of these was deaf and dumb, one was blind, and one lacked a leg.

'Good afternoon, my dear brethren,' said Little John to the other three. 'Glad am I to come upon so many of my own kind. I hope you have had better fortune today in the begging trade than I have had?'

'Greetings, brother,' said the lame man. 'We have fared as well as we could hope, but yet we are beggars even as yourself, with scarce a penny piece between us.'

'You have a villain and a traitor amongst you,' said Little John, pointing to the beggar who was wearing his clothes. 'That is no beggar, but a robber!'

'I am as true a beggar as the rest,' shouted the first beggar jumping to his feet. 'And as well known as such from Berwick to Dover. It is this fellow who is the traitor and outlaw. Help me, good friends, and we'll string him up to the nearest tree.'

But Little John was so mad with rage that his first blow laid the beggar on the ground before him – and he proceeded to give him the best thrashing he had ever had in his life.

Then he turned to the other three beggars, to find that they had drawn swords and knives and were about to attack him from behind.

'Ah-ha!' cried Little John. 'More knaves to be beaten, are there!'

With that he knocked down the deaf-and-dumb beggar, and beat him until he shouted for mercy.

'A miracle!' laughed Little John. 'The dumb speaks! Let me try whether the blind can see!' He aimed a blow at the blind beggar, who had again come creeping up behind him with a long knife in his hand – and the fellow dodged the staff, only to be knocked head over heels with a blow from the other end of it.

Seeing this the one-legged beggar hastily let down his left leg, which was strapped up behind, and started to run away on two completely unmaimed limbs.

'More miracles!' shouted Little John, and with a few strides he overtook this beggar also and brought him to the ground.

Then having disarmed all four and tied their hands firmly behind them, Little John retrieved his own clothes and changed them for the filthy old coats and hats.

'I'll give up being a beggar,' he said gravely, 'my fortune has been so good today. Ah-ha, I heard the gold ring when I thrashed each one of you!'

So saying he ransacked the pockets, pouches, and bags of each beggar in turn, and counted out more than three hundred pounds in gold, most of this being hidden among the meal in the great bag worn by the first beggar he and Robin had met.

'A good harvest,' said Little John. 'I have threshed my sheaves to some purpose – and they have indeed yielded golden grain! Stay you all here and mend your ways in future. I am off to make report to bold Robin Hood – who is indeed King of Sherwood.'

At the trysting tree in the secret glade Little John found Robin and a great throng of the outlaws sitting down to supper round the great fires.

'Greetings, good master!' he cried gaily. 'How fared you as a beggar? Not better than I, I dare swear. For look you what I have got by my begging: three hundred pounds in gold!'

And with that he told the tale of the four beggars, amid laughter and cheers.

'I am glad that insolent rogue got him a good thrashing,' said Robin. 'For he was a low thief, and no honest beggar. But my gains are greater than yours, Little John. For see, as a beggar, I won three men's lives – and here they are, three proper young men to draw a bow and strike a blow for freedom, for right, and for King Richard!'

All applauded this speech, and Little John was the first to admit that Robin had indeed proved the better beggar that day and won a more valuable booty than any hoard of gold.

CHAPTER THIRTEEN

ROBIN HOOD AND THE TANNER

In Nottingham there lives a jolly tanner,
His name is Arthur-a-Bland;
There is nere a squire in Nottinghamshire
Dare bid bold Arthur stand.
    BALLAD: *Robin Hood and the Tanner*

WHILE Robin Hood gained many new followers by
rescuing them from the cruelty of the Forest Laws or the
tyranny of men like Guy of Gisborne and the Sheriff of
Nottingham, many more came to seek him and offer
their services as his fame grew greater.

But sometimes, as in the cases of Little John and
Gilbert-of-the-White-Hand, Robin went out and won a
new follower after testing his prowess in single combat –
rather as King Arthur's knights had done.

After Little John and Gilbert the most notable of
these was Arthur-a-Bland, the yeoman whom Sir Richard of Legh had rescued at the archery contest in
Barnsdale. Arthur was by profession a tanner, and he
rode about the country trading in skins – buying them
green from farmer or forester, and selling them again,
beautifully cured and dressed, to rich merchants or even
to knights and their ladies.

On one such expedition he was riding along the high
road to Nottingham when he met with Robin Hood.

Robin was wearing brown and green and carrying no
bow but only a quarter-staff, passing himself off as a
yeoman in search of work either as a farmer or a forester.

It was a lovely May day, and Arthur was singing as he went:

> *In summer when the woods are bright*
> *And leaves be large and long,*
> *It is full merry in fair forest*
> *To hear the small birds' song.*

Then Robin joined in, singing the second verse by himself:

> *To see the deer draw to the dale*
> *And leave the hills' high lea*
> *And shadow them in the leaves so green*
> *Under the greenwood tree.*

And they both sang the third verse together:

> *It befell at Whitsuntide*
> *Early in a May morning,*
> *The sun up fair began to shine*
> *And merrily birds to sing.*

'Well met, jolly fellow, well met!' cried Robin.

'And well met too on this day of song!' answered Arthur-a-Bland.

'You are a tanner, I take it?' said Robin, turning and walking beside the other's horse. 'Ah, sad news indeed have I heard concerning a new law against all tanners.'

'New law? Sad news?' Arthur-a-Bland's face fell and he looked suddenly anxious.

'All tanners who drink too much ale and beer are to be set in the stocks,' declared Robin, keeping a straight face with difficulty.

'Drinking ale and beer!' roared Arthur, nearly falling off his horse with laughter. 'By the mass, you'll lose no freedom by that.'

'Oh yes you will,' said Robin. 'You'll lose the freedom of your legs. That is the law – of Nature!'

'It is a freedom I'll wager that you lose sooner than I do!' laughed Arthur.

'I'll take your wager,' said Robin. 'Let us on to Nottingham. . . . But tell me, what brings you by this forest road?'

'A good ploy,' said Arthur, 'a new line of trade, ha-ha! There is a great reward offered for the capture of a bold, bad outlaw called Robin Hood. I have in my pocket a warrant for his arrest signed by the Sheriff of Nottingham. Why should I starve my way about the country buying and selling stinking skins, when by catching one mangy outlaw I might earn five hundred pounds?'

'Why indeed!' agreed Robin.

'If you can help me to this capture,' went on Arthur, 'I'll pay you well out of my reward. A hundred pounds, now: how would that be?'

'Let me see your warrant,' said Robin cautiously. 'If it be well and truly drawn out, I will do the best I can to give you the chance you seek.'

'No, no,' answered Arthur. 'I'll trust it into no hand but mine own. I'll have no man coming between me and my reward.'

'Have it as you will,' said Robin. 'But let us make our bargain too. If I bring you where you may find this Robin Hood alone, unarmed and at your mercy, will you promise to pay me a hundred pounds?'

'That I will,' answered Arthur eagerly, and bound himself to it by a great oath.

'Let us go to Nottingham then,' said Robin. 'I know of an inn on the edge of the forest where Robin Hood is often to be found. Indeed I can guarantee that he'll be there today.'

Off they went accordingly, and before long came to the inn, where Robin managed to put in a secret word with the innkeeper while ordering both ale and wine.

'I have no weapon. You have a sword . . . what about
that hundred pounds!'

'We'll drink, shall we not, while waiting for our man?'
said Robin. And Arthur agreed eagerly.

Very soon he showed that Robin's joke about tanners
was no more than the truth: the more wine and ale they
called for, the more Arthur drank, and before long his
legs had indeed lost their freedom, and he found it diffi-
cult to sit up even upon the floor.

'Now, my fine fellow,' said Robin. 'You see me here, I have no weapon but a staff – and that leans over there against the wall. You, on the other hand, have a sword by your side, and the Sheriff's warrant in your pocket. . . . Now then, what about that hundred pounds?'

But Arthur-a-Bland only stared stupidly at him for a moment, and then fell slowly over on his side and lay there snoring loudly.

Robin undid his pouch and searched it. There he found only the warrant and ten silver pieces – so he left all there except the warrant, and taking up his staff walked quietly out of the inn, after a few more words with his friend the inn keeper.

Presently Arthur-a-Bland woke from his drunken slumbers, sat up, groaned, and after looking in his pouch, called for the inn keeper.

'I have been robbed in your inn,' he lamented. 'I had here a warrant from the Sheriff of Nottingham that would have made my fortune: it was to capture a bold outlaw called Robin Hood. But now both warrant and reward are lost – and he that I thought my friend has robbed me of them.'

'Why!' cried the inn keeper with well-feigned surprise. 'Did you not know that this friend of yours who was here only a little while since was none other than Robin Hood himself?'

'Robin Hood!' gasped Arthur. 'Oh, he has tricked me handsomely! Had I but known! Well, I'll not stay here while he escapes. Which way did he go?'

'Along the road into the forest,' answered the inn-keeper. 'And before you go, there is the little matter of the wine and ale that you and your friend have drunk. . . . Ten shillings is what you owe me, and if you do not pay, I'll lock you in my cellar until I can take you before the Justices.'

Sighing deeply, Arthur paid out all the money in his pouch, and then vowing a terrible vengeance on Robin Hood, he sprang up on his horse and cantered off into the forest.

It was late in the afternoon when he came up with Robin, who was striding along the road, swinging his staff and singing merrily.

'Stand, you villain!' bellowed Arthur. 'Yield yourself up, or I'll cut your head open with my sword!'

'What knave have we here?' asked Robin, turning round and raising his staff.

'No knave,' answered Arthur fiercely, 'and that you shall soon know!'

'Why, it's my friend the tanner!' cried Robin. 'Welcome, my dear friend, welcome! Doubtless you have come to pay me the hundred pounds you owe me.'

'Hundred pounds!' gasped Arthur, purple with fury.

'That was the sum,' replied Robin gravely. 'You promised it to me if I delivered Robin Hood to you unarmed and alone. Well, I did even so at the inn: for I myself am Robin. . . . But I think you were suffering under the tanners' law of which I told you – for you showed no signs of rising up to arrest me!'

'I'll arrest you now, fast enough!' shouted Arthur, and springing from his horse he drew his sword and rushed upon Robin – who, with a quick blow of his staff, sent it flying from his hand.

'Fight fair,' said Robin. 'Go, cut you a staff such as mine, and we'll see who is to do the arresting this day!'

Trembling with rage, Arthur-a-Bland rushed to the nearest thicket, cut himself a good oaken staff, and attacked Robin with such vigour that the crack and clatter of wood on wood echoed up and down the forest glades.

Once they paused for breath, and Robin remarked:

'I think, friend, that my staff is longer than yours. Would you like me to measure them, and cut mine to your length?'

'It matters not,' said Arthur. 'Mine's a good eight feet of oak such as I use for knocking out a calf – and I'm sure it's quite long enough to knock you out also!'

Then they went at it again, and very soon blood was trickling down both their faces. Robin raged round like a wild boar that has tasted blood, but Arthur stood in one place and laid on with his staff just as if he were a woodman splitting a log.

For nearly two hours they kept at it, exchanging many a hit, while the wood rang with the blows of staff on staff.

'Come, hold your hand,' panted Robin at last. 'Let us end the quarrel. For neither of us will gain much by threshing the others' bones into a bran-mash.'

'I hunger still for my five hundred pounds,' gasped Arthur. 'Indeed, I must earn them, or I cannot pay the hundred which I owe to you!'

'Come and join my merry band in Sherwood,' said Robin. 'I'll promise that you'll earn much more than five hundred pounds there – though I'll see to it that you pay me your debt!'

Arthur-a-Bland still hesitated. 'I am a free man,' he said, 'and a tanner of note. I made sure to tan your hide – and sell it to the Sheriff!'

'Well, at least come and dine with us,' said Robin. 'I owe you a good meal in exchange for the good drink I had at your expense. But I hope that you will remain with us: for I hear that you are a notable archer, and I bear on my sides the proof that you are a notable wielder of the staff!'

Robin then blew his horn, and before long Little John and several others appeared among the trees.

'By the Mass!' exclaimed Arthur. 'Is that not John Little whom I see coming over yonder?'

'That was his name,' answered Robin, 'before he suffered a forest change and became my dearest friend and most faithful follower as Little John.'

'Then I am with you indeed,' cried Arthur. 'John is my own cousin, our mothers being sisters, and I have ever loved him like a brother. And I have been seeking him these several years.'

'What is the matter, good master?' called Little John as he drew near and saw the blood on Robin's face.

'This fine tanner has been tanning my hide for me!' answered Robin with a grin.

'He is to be commended,' said Little John gravely, 'for few can do that. But if he is so stout a fellow, let me have a bout with him and see if he can tan my hide also!'

'Hold your hand, good John,' said Robin. 'Here has been fighting enough. This our new companion is called Arthur-a-Bland . . . I believe that you know him!'

Then Arthur and Little John flung their staffs away and clasped one another, almost weeping with joy. And when Arthur had sworn to be loyal and true in all his dealings with Robin Hood and the rest of the Sherwood outlaws, Robin took an arm of each and led them away towards the secret glade to eat, drink, and make merry over their new alliance. And as they went through the tuneful woods they sang gaily:

> *Oh ever hereafter as long as we live*
> *We three will be as one:*
> *The wood it shall ring and the minstrel shall sing*
> *Of Robin Hood, Arthur, and John!*

CHAPTER FOURTEEN

THE WEDDING OF ALLIN-A-DALE

Who gives me this maid? said Little John.
Quoth Robin Hood, That do I;
And he that takes her from Allin-a-Dale,
Full dearly he shall her buy.

BALLAD: *Robin Hood and Allin-a-Dale*

ALTHOUGH Robin Hood and his men lived mainly in the caves and huts of the secret glade in the wildest depths of Sherwood Forest, they had many other dwelling places as well. And these were not merely in the other forests which covered so much of the north of England at that time.

There were one or two knights such as Sir Richard of Legh, ardent followers of King Richard and enemies of Prince John, who were ever ready to entertain or shelter Robin or any of his followers. There was also many and many another home of a poorer sort where any of the band were sure of welcome and protection – and certain that no treachery would find them: for though a price was set on every one of their heads, even the poorest serf would have died rather than betray them.

Many of these secret friends had been saved from death or want by Robin and his men: one, the minstrel Allin-a-Dale, owed Robin a debt of another kind.

Robin saw him first one spring day as he stood in the pale green shade of a chestnut tree waiting to shoot one of the dappled deer.

There came a sound of a merry singing, and a brave

young man came tripping along a forest path, as fine a
sight as could be seen. He was clothed in scarlet red –
scarlet both fine and gay, and as he strode along, springing a little with each step, he sang as sweetly as a bird:

> *Lent is come with love to town*
> *With blossom and with birds aroun'*
> *That all bliss bringeth.*
> *Daisies grow in every dale,*
> *Sweet notes of the nightingale,*
> *And each bird singeth.*

And ever and anon he paused to strike a trilling melody
from the little harp which hung from his shoulder.

Next day Robin saw him again – but different quite
from what he had been. Now he came drooping through
the woods, his feet dragging, his head bent. Gone was
the fine array of scarlet red, and instead of the merry
song he twanged a doleful dirge upon his harp and sang
of lost love and hope cast away.

At a sign from Robin, Little John and Much stepped
out into the open and barred the young man's way: but
he drew his sword quickly and stood in a posture of
defence.

'Stand off! Stand off!' he cried. 'What is your will
with me?'

'You must come before our master at once,' said
Much. 'He awaits you in the wood yonder.'

'And who is your master?' asked Allin-a-Dale.

'Robin Hood.'

'Why then I'll come. He is a good man, and means no
harm to a poor minstrel.'

When he was brought to him Robin asked courteously:

'Fair sir, have you any money to spare for my merry
men and me?'

'I have no money at all,' was the answer, 'except for five shillings, and a ring. These I have hoarded seven long years to have at my wedding. Yesterday I should have married the fairest maid in all the world – but she was taken away from me, and they are forcing her to marry a rich old knight: therefore my heart is broken.'

'What is your name?' asked Robin.

'Allin-a-Dale,' was the answer. 'A poor minstrel, though I can sing and play – and shoot too if needs be, and wield a sword as well as any man.'

'And what will you give me,' asked Robin, 'if I deliver your true love from the old knight and return her safely to you?'

'Alas,' said Allin, 'I have no money. But I will swear upon the Bible to be your true and faithful servant.'

'How many miles is it to where your true love is?' asked Robin. 'See that you tell me exactly.'

'By my faith,' said Allin eagerly, 'it is not more than five miles.'

Then after speaking a word or two with Little John, Robin borrowed Allin's harp, wrapped his cloak about him, and set out as fast as he could walk until he came to the church where the wedding was to be.

When he got there he found everyone waiting for the bride and bridegroom, and the Bishop of Peterborough who was to perform the ceremony asked him who he was and why he came pushing his way into the church.

'I am the best harper in the north country,' answered Robin boldly. 'And I am sure that no wedding is complete without music.'

'If that is so, you are right welcome,' said the Bishop. 'Come, play to us until bride and groom arrive.'

So Robin played a number of simple, merry country tunes, and everyone was contented – until the bride arrived.

She was both young and lovely, but as pale as death and her eyes red with weeping.

After her came the old knight who was to be her husband – an evil-looking old man who shuffled along, his chin wagging with palsy, his eyes leering at the pretty young girl who was being sold to him – for the marriage was nothing else.

Robin ought to have ceased from his harping
when the bridegroom came

Now Robin ought to have ceased from his harping when the bridegroom came, but instead of that, he played louder and louder.

'Silence now, silence master harper!' cried the Bishop angrily.

'Not so,' answered Robin calmly. 'For I see no bridegroom yet for this lovely lass who shines like glittering gold with her youth and beauty. . . . This old man is, I suppose, her grandfather, come to give her in marriage to the man of her choice?'

'Impudent fellow!' spluttered the Bishop. 'This is my brother, and he is to marry the girl!'

'Is he your own choice?' asked Robin turning to the bride, and sadly she murmured 'No.'

'It is not for her to choose!' shouted the Bishop. 'Her parents are dead, and I, as her legal guardian, say that she shall marry my brother. She had some silly, girlish fancy for a penniless minstrel called Allin-a-Dale; but I sent him to the right-about yesterday, and he'll not return. A knight's daughter with house and lands in her own right is not for such as he!'

'Ah-ha!' cried Robin. 'So that's it! There's money behind it – and a Judas masquerading as a Bishop!'

With that he set his horn to his lips and blew a long shrill call; and the echoes had not died away before a band of more than two dozen archers came pouring into the church. And at their head was Allin-a-Dale, and it was he who reached Robin first and placed a bow in his hands.

'And now,' said Robin sternly, 'let the marriage proceed – but with the lawful bridegroom. Lawful, according to the law of God!'

'Here am I,' said Allin-a-Dale.

'Good,' replied Robin. 'You come a bachelor, but you shall leave this church a married man!'

'It shall not be!' stormed the Bishop. 'It can be no lawful marriage: the banns must be called three times – that is the law of England.'

'Little John,' commanded Robin, 'find you a gown and a surplice, go up into the pulpit, and call the banns!'

Little John helped himself to a gown from a minor

priest, a surplice from the Bishop himself, and ascended the steps with solemn mien, while Robin murmured:

'By my faith, this cloth makes a different man of him!'

But Little John was not turned suddenly into a priest, and he made everyone in the church laugh by calling the banns seven times 'lest,' as he explained, 'three times should not be enough!'

Neither the Bishop nor the old knight dared forbid the banns, for Robin set an arrow in his bowstring and glanced at them threateningly.

'Who giveth this maid to be married?' asked Little John.

'That do I!' cried Robin. 'And he who tries to take her from Allin-a-Dale must beware of Robin Hood! And any one who tries to defraud her of land or money needs to beware of me also!'

After this, Little John came down from the pulpit and returned his robe to the Bishop.

'Now then, my lord Bishop,' said Robin sternly, 'we wait for you to perform the ceremony according to the full rites of Holy Church.'

'I will not do it!' growled the Bishop.

'No?' said Robin slowly. 'Then we will fetch our own priest, Friar Tuck, from the forest. . . . But you, my lord Bishop, may expect a visit from several hundred of my men – who will collect a clerk's fee from you to the extent of all you possess.'

After that the Bishop married Allin-a-Dale to the bride, who looked like a queen, her eyes shining with happiness.

And in the course of time she and Allin-a-Dale were able to secure her father's house and lands on the borders of Sherwood Forest, and live there untroubled in their peace and happiness.

Moreover so long as he lived Robin Hood was the most welcome guest who ever came there, and many were the songs and ballads that Allin made about the doings of him and his merry men.

CHAPTER FIFTEEN

ROBIN HOOD AND THE BISHOP

Come, gentlemen all, and listen awhile,
And a story I'll to you unfold;
I'll tell you how Robin Hood served the bishop
When he robbed him of his gold.

BALLAD: *Robin Hood and the Bishop*

THE BISHOP OF PETERBOROUGH was not a man who would easily forgive Robin Hood for outwitting him in the affair of Allin-a-Dale, and he sought for revenge most eagerly.

He went first to the Sheriff of Nottingham.

'Master Sheriff,' he said, 'I demand a company of men at arms and archers to punish this villain Robin Hood!'

'My Lord Bishop,' answered the Sheriff, 'I would willingly do anything I might to scatter these bold outlaws and hang Robin Hood. I myself have many reasons for wishing to be revenged on him. But I cannot gather a large enough company: all men hereabouts seem to be in league with him.'

'Then I will visit the knights and the barons of this shire,' stormed the Bishop. '*They* will not be in league with this traitor!'

'You will get little help from them,' answered the Sheriff sadly. 'The lesser knights will scarcely dare to attack him, lest he should burn down their steads and drive away their flocks and herds.'

'But the barons?' persisted the Bishop. 'A few wild

ruffians in the forest will scarcely burn down a well-fortified castle!'

'Robin Hood's band is said to exceed three hundred men in number,' answered the Sheriff. 'As for the barons, assuredly they will assist you – and call out all their liegemen and tenants and serfs: but, however big an army they collect, you will never find Robin Hood by their aid. Oh, you'll never be able to accuse a single man of them of treachery – but Robin Hood will have had due warning, and he and his whole gang will be settled quietly in Barnsdale or Plompton or Delamere or Pendle before ever your expedition sets out.'

'Then what can I do?' fumed the Bishop.

'Take him by surprise,' answered the Sheriff. 'Go with a small company of my men. Sir Guy of Gisborne would help you, only he is away fighting for Prince John, so I will lend you my seneschal Worman. He was Robin Hood's steward, and hates his former master. Take him and twenty or thirty men. Doubtless the wily Worman will hatch a scheme for you. . . .'

Robin wandered in the forest to shoot a deer, when he met with a palmer – a silly old man dressed in ragged clothes and hung about with bags like a beggar.

'Ah, sir!' cried the palmer in a high, cracked voice; 'you look like a forest man: can you tell me where I may find Robin Hood? Oh, he's a kind man, a noble man, is bold Robin!'

'How now, you silly fellow,' said Robin, 'what's the news? What is it that you want to tell Robin Hood so badly?'

'A fearful thing! Such a to-do!' cackled the palmer. 'Master Sheriff's seneschal, Master Worman, is dealing out the Forest Laws with four men to help him. Oh, such a shame, such a crying shame! Three proper young men – and two will hang, and the third grope his way blind till God releases him from life.'

'Where?' asked Robin briskly.

'Not a furlong hence,' answered the palmer. 'You know the cottage by the brook? Well over the slope beyond . . . One of the lads is the old woman's son.'

'How near to the hanging are they?' asked Robin.

'Oh, they wait awhile, for the hangman has not come.'

'Good,' said Robin. 'Now make haste, old man, and lend me your gown. Here are forty shillings in payment for it.'

'Ah, my gown is in rags,' piped the old palmer. 'You do but jest! . . . Oh, sir, you will not rob an old man?'

'Content,' exclaimed Robin curtly. 'Here is the money. Strip off that gown quickly. And know that I myself am Robin Hood.'

'Oh then indeed, noble sir, I know that you will deal justly with me,' cried the palmer, and he stripped off his gown with great alacrity.

Robin put it on – a strange garment, patched with black, blue, and red, on which hung the various bags like pockets turned inside out, in which the palmer put the food which was given to him. Then he put on the palmer's dirty, frayed old hat, and set off through the forest as fast as he could go.

Past the old woman's cottage he went, over the stream by the stepping stones, and over the brow of the slope beyond. There, sure enough, were several Forest guards or Verderers standing round a newly lighted fire. By them stood Worman holding the reins of his horse, and from a tree nearby a man was hanging, his limbs yet jerking though he was already dead.

'Too easy a death,' Worman was saying, with a harsh laugh. 'The jerk as I led the horse away from under him broke his neck and he died in a moment. Now if we had but a proper hangman to pull the other rogue up gently and throttle the life out of him slowly as he struggles at the rope's end . . .'

'God save you, master forester!' cackled Robin, hobbling up at this moment, dressed as the old palmer. 'Did I hear your highness say that you were in need of a hangman this day?'

'You did, old man,' said Worman shortly.

'What will you give me as a hangman's fee if I do the job for you?'

'A new suit of clothes – which you sorely need,' said Worman. 'And a piece of gold if you will blind this other miserable law-breaker for us.'

'Give me but iron and rope!' cried Robin, 'and I'll show you how clever I am at the job!'

'Give them to him,' ordered Worman.

As soon as Robin had the halter and the blinding-iron in his hand, he leapt swiftly onto a fallen stump nearby, and climbed into a spreading oak-tree.

'By my head, you're a nimble old man!' remarked Worman, with a grin. 'Make haste and fasten the rope, for I know of a traitor who has lived too long!'

'I was never a hangman in my life,' said Robin, still in the palmer's voice, 'nor do I intend to be now. Cursed be all who consent to be of such a trade!'

'How now, what mean you?' asked Worman anxiously.

'Ha-ha!' cried Robin, and he sang:

> *I've a bag for meal and a bag for malt,*
> *And a bag for barley and corn;*
> *A bag for bread, and a bag for beef –*
> *And a bag for my little small horn!*

So saying, he pulled out his horn, and blew a piercingly shrill note on it.

'Wind away!' laughed Worman. 'You silly old palmer, I know you well. Blow till your eyes drop out – it will but deprive me of the pleasure of burning them!'

Even as he said this, Robin was aware of armed men wearing the Sheriff's livery who were closing in round the tree, and of the Bishop of Peterborough with his followers riding through the forest towards where he was.

'A trap!' thought Robin, and in a moment he had dropped out of the tree and was running his hardest down the hill while Worman shouted:

'After him, men! It is Robin Hood! This time he cannot escape!'

Robin bounded across the stepping stones and flung himself against the cottage door, which flew open at a touch.

'God-a-mercy!' screamed the old woman. 'Who ever are you!'

'Peace, good mother!' gasped Robin. 'You know me well – I am Robin Hood. And yonder is the Bishop of Peterborough and the Sheriff's men: I cannot get away, and if they take me, I'll hang before your door!'

'That shall never be!' cried the old woman. 'I mind me of how you saved my boy once from losing his arrow fingers – and the many a time you have brought me food when I was starving. . . . But I knew you not in that strange guise. . . .'

'I've no time to tell you of it,' began Robin.

'Quick,' interrupted the old woman. 'Change clothes with me – your Lincoln green as well as that gown. By God's grace he'll not want to hang you here, but to take you off to Nottingham . . .'

Swiftly the exchange was made, and when the first soldier reached the door and burst it open, Robin was busily cooking over the fire – a perfect old woman in the dim light of the cottage.

Robin was busily cooking over the fire

'Where is that traitor Robin Hood?' cried the leader of the men, who was none other than Worman.

'Robin Hood?' screeched the old woman who was really Robin. 'What do I know of him?'

'Search the place,' commanded Worman briefly, and it did not take many minutes to find the old woman dressed as Robin Hood, and drag her out into the open.

'Ah-ha, you false traitor!' cried Worman exultantly. 'We have you fast at length. I've long lived in fear of you, and today that fear is ended. But you shall have an hour or two in which to fear me – while I am heating the irons to burn out your eyes, which I shall do with my own hand. But that of course will come after I have cut off those fingers, with which you pull a bowstring and break the Forest Laws. ... And maybe even a bowstring for the halter which hangs you would be but justice. ...'

'Is that the proud traitor Robin Hood?' asked the Bishop, riding up at that moment.

'Here he is, safe enough, my lord,' answered Worman. 'Our little trap worked splendidly as you see. Ah, I knew how to snare this rascal.'

'A rich reward shall be yours, Master Worman,' said the Bishop. 'Set the villain on a horse, tie him with his face towards the tail, and let us hasten away to Nottingham.'

When this was done they rode gently up the slope again, the Bishop laughing and joking in his delight at capturing Robin Hood, until they came to the tree where Worman's first victim was hanging.

'Faugh!' said the Bishop. 'This tree bears strange fruit! But tell me, master seneschal, was this all a blind to catch Robin Hood?'

'Not so,' answered Worman. 'That carrion had killed three of King John's deer – '

'*King* John?' queried the Bishop, but with a sly smile.

'King John!' declared Worman. 'For surely Richard is dead. ... And that reminds me, we have two other criminals, one to hang and one to lose his eyes. We'd better hang them both quickly, as it is not good to delay here with so dangerous a prisoner as Robin Hood. ... You, master verderer, send one of your men up the tree to fix a couple of ropes. Tie the villains' hands and set them on my horse's saddle in turn. ... If I whistle my horse will come to me – and there we have a hangman where no hangman is!'

So the ropes were fixed, and the first man made to stand on Worman's horse with the noose round his neck and his hands bound.

'And now,' said Worman, deliberately enjoying his victim's fear, 'I am about to whistle for my horse. He will obey me ... sooner or later.'

But as he ended there came a whistle of another kind, and an arrow sped over their heads and severed the rope clean through. Then the young man who had so narrowly been saved from hanging dropped astride the horse, kicked it fiercely with his heels, and galloped away, his hands still bound behind him.

'Who shot yonder arrow?' began the Bishop, and then he turned pale and his jaw fell. For out of the forest on every side came archers in Lincoln green, running company by company, the arrows ready on their bows.

'Marry!' cried the old woman with a shrill scream of laughter, 'I think it must be a man they call Robin Hood! Yes, there he comes at the head of his merry men.'

'Robin Hood!' gasped the Bishop, while Worman turned a sickly green and trembled so that he nearly fell. 'Then in the devil's name, who and what are you?'

'Why, you wicked Bishop, I am but a poor old woman – as plain you may see if you strip off these garments, which Robin Hood gave me of his charity!'

'Then woe is me,' said the Bishop, 'that ever I saw this day!'

But Worman turned to his men. 'Fire a volley of arrows!' he shouted. 'Then draw your swords and fight like men! Fight, curse you!'

But the Sheriff's men flung down their bows and fled for dear life, the ranks of the outlaws opening to let them pass, and closing again when they were gone.

Then Robin strode up to where Worman and the Bishop sat their horses, pale and trembling, with only two of the Bishop's followers who, as priests, hoped that they did not need to fly for their lives.

'Come,' said the Bishop hastily. 'Let us away. He will not dare to risk the curse of Holy Church!'

'Hold, Bishop!' cried Robin sternly. 'I mean you no harm, and you must dine with me before you go. . . . But I have justice to perform first. John, Scarlet, Arthur, seize Worman and bind his hands.'

Then Worman flung himself on the ground, weeping and praying for mercy.

'Spare me, noble Huntingdon!' he howled. 'I served you long and faithfully – '

'Until it served your turn better to betray me,' interrupted Robin coldly. 'Yes, deny it not. . . . That I forgave you, and sought for no vengeance. But you yourself have shown no mercy, though mercy has been shown to you, and you swore to me once as Scarlet did also, to do all in your power to save whom you could from the cruel Forest Laws which bring God's curse upon this poor land. . . . No, no words. . . . Here, one of you, fling a rope over that branch. . . . Good, now the noose over his head. . . . Friar Tuck, the last rites of the Church – then six of you run away with the end of the rope and make it fast . . .'

When Worman had met the fate he so richly deserved Robin Hood turned to the Bishop.

'Now come you to dinner, my lord,' he said courteously.

'I would rather die,' shouted the Bishop.

'Why then,' said Robin, 'you may ride away – after you have paid toll.'

So saying he spread his cloak on the ground, and a

search of the Bishop's pockets and saddle bags soon supplied it with a shining pile of gold and silver.

Meanwhile the Bishop, cursing him in English and
Latin, was tied to a tree.

'Let him go now,' commanded Robin, pouring the
money into several bags.

'Not yet,' said Little John. 'It is rarely that we have
so high a dignitary of the Church as a guest. Let him
sing Mass for us before he goes.'

'I would rather die,' repeated the Bishop sulkily.

'Then you may do so,' said Robin, 'for there you stay,
tied to that tree, until you fulfil your duty as a priest.'

Then the Bishop sang Mass, assisted by his two
trembling followers, while all the outlaws doffed their
hoods and knelt reverently round about him.

'I thank you, my lord Bishop,' said Robin gravely
when the service was ended. 'Now go in peace.'

So he cut the Bishop's bonds, set him on his horse, and
guided him carefully back to the main road which led to
Nottingham.

CHAPTER SIXTEEN

GEORGE-A-GREENE, THE PINNER
OF WAKEFIELD

The first whereof that I intend to show
Is merry Wakefield, and her pinner too,
Which fame hath blazed with all that did belong
Unto that town in many gladsome song,
The pinner's valour, and how firm he stood
In th' town's defence 'gainst th' rebel Robin Hood.

RICHARD BRATHWAYTE: *A Strappado for the Divell* (1615)

THE years went by quickly enough while Robin Hood dwelt in Sherwood with his merry band of outlaws. Outside in the greater world Prince John plotted and schemed to gain power, and King Richard after his unsuccessful Crusade was captured by the Archduke of Austria and languished long in prison. Rumours of Richard's fate crept home to England, which John strove to turn to his own good; but Blondel, Richard's faithful minstrel friend, sought him all over Europe, found him in his castle prison, and brought back the news.

Then, though John strove to discredit it, the truth was told throughout England, and rich and poor alike brought what money they could towards the great ransom which the Archduke demanded for their King.

Robin Hood was very active in the collecting of this ransom, and no bishop or abbot, nor any baron, knight, or even squire who was known to be a follower of Prince John, could pass through Sherwood Forest without being stopped for tribute.

But while the ransom was collecting, John strove once more to seize the crown for himself, and there was great unrest particularly in the North of England where many barons favoured him, but Ranulph Earl of Chester stood staunchly for King Richard and strove to catch and kill as traitors any who stood for Prince John.

A humbler champion of King Richard's, but one who has won to even greater fame was a certain George-a-Greene who was the Pinner of Wakefield in Yorkshire. His profession was to catch any sheep or cattle found straying on the roads or in the fields of corn or hay and pound them – that is shut them up until claimed (with an appropriate fine) in the village pound or pinfold which was like a small pen or run with high stone walls and a strong gate.

George-a-Greene, however, pounded traitors as well as cattle, defied even the commanders who came to attack the little town of Wakefield with their troops of men at arms and archers, and won victory after victory with the aid of the men of Wakefield, until on a sudden his name was more talked of throughout the country than even that of Robin Hood.

George was a man of great strength and he was skilled with all weapons. Naturally all the maidens of Wakefield sought his love, and the most beautiful of them all, Bettris, the daughter of a wealthy Justice called Grimes, won his heart. For a long time, however, Grimes would not allow them to marry: he himself was rather inclined towards Prince John's side, and a great lord among the rebels sought Bettris's hand in marriage.

George won Grimes's consent at length, but only after many setbacks and adventures which were noised abroad and even sung of in ballads to such an extent that Bettris was soon as famous throughout the land as George-a-Greene himself.

Rumours of all this reached Robin and his men in Sherwood, but most was told them by a wandering minstrel who was sheltered in the secret dell during a fortnight of heavy rain. He strove to pay for his entertainment by telling stories and singing ballads, and it chanced that most of these were concerned with the bravery and strength of George-a-Greene, and the unparalleled beauty of the lovely Bettris.

When the minstrel had gone, Robin noticed that Marian was strangely silent and depressed, and her melancholy and shortness of temper grew so extreme that he was almost inclined to fear lest he had cause for jealousy.

'My lovely Marian,' said he one April day as they sat near to one another by the great trysting tree in the secret glade. 'Why are you not cheerful as you used to be? What ails you, my sweetheart, and makes you so sad? Is it this long, long wait for Richard to come home to his own and give you to me in marriage, according to our oath?'

Marian smiled, and leant her head against Robin's arm.

'No, no!' she said softly. 'Though indeed I long more and more for that happy day,' and she sighed a little.

'What is it, then, sweetheart?'

'You must not laugh at me, Robin,' she said, looking half-ashamed as she spoke. 'I think these long days of wet spring after snowy winter when there is little I can do – I think they are largely to blame: surely otherwise I would not worry about so trifling a care.'

She paused, and Robin said tenderly:

'Dear heart, you know well that no care of yours can seem a trifle to me. Tell on, I pray you.'

'Well,' answered Marian hesitatingly, 'one hears more and more these days of the deeds and the valour of this George-a-Greene, and of the beauty of his love the fair Bettris who is said to exceed all women in her loveliness. Until lately, your name, my Robin, was on everyone's lips and in all the songs of the minstrels and pedlars, and they told of your deeds of prowess, your skill with bow or with quarter-staff, and – and of Maid Marian the Queen of Sherwood.'

'And so they shall again!' declared Robin. 'This fellow is an upstart and rides to fame on a bubble reputation which will burst sooner or later – albeit he is a good man and a loyal, from all I hear. . . . As for this Bettris of his, I'll wager my head that could you but be seen once in her company, no one would look at her again!'

'Then can we not go to Wakefield,' hesitated Marian. 'I cannot bear to think that men say George-a-Greene could beat Robin Hood with the quarter-staff.'

'Content, content!' laughed Robin Hood. 'We will away to Wakefield forthwith! The Spring is upon us, and I feel ready for any mad adventure. Like you I also have been cooped up in our caves far too long. . . . Yes, we will dress you as a forester – the very garb in which you deceived me when you came to seek me here. And we will take with us but Scarlet and John. Let us tell them of our venture, and bid them make sure that their bowstrings are strong, their arrows keen – and their staffs of the toughest oak. I'll warrant heads will be broken when we meet with George-a-Greene!'

Not many evenings later, his cares permitting, George-a-Greene walked forth into the country outside Wakefield with Bettris on his arm, to view the fields where the lately sown corn was already showing tender green shoots above the brown earth.

'Tell me, sweet love,' George was saying, 'are you indeed content to wed with so simple a man as I, when knights and gentlemen seek your hand in marriage?'

'Were you as strong as Robin Hood of Sherwood, still you
have no right to walk across the corn'

'Oh, George, how can you so doubt my love –'
began Bettris, and then stopped suddenly, for George-a-
Greene was grasping his staff, flushed with anger, and
gazing across the nearest field.

'Look!' he exclaimed. 'There are four men breaking
through the hedge. Yes, they are coming straight towards us across the corn. Oh, this is not to be borne!'
Then raising his voice, he roared out:

'Get back, you foolish travellers! You are wrong –
you must not come that way!'

'Now by my soul,' answered the foremost, who was dressed like all of them in Lincoln green and carried a staff in his hand. 'By my soul, proud sir, we be four brave foresters, and you but one puny yeoman – who are you to tell us which way to go?'

'Get back quickly,' shouted George, 'or I will make you skip over hedge and ditch, I'll warrant you. What, is not the highway good enough for you that you must make a path over the new corn?'

'Are you mad?' cried Robin, who was of course the leader of the four. 'Dare you encounter four such men as we? We are no babes, man, just look at our limbs!'

'Sirrah,' answered George, 'the biggest limbs have not always the stoutest hearts. Were you as strong as Robin Hood of Sherwood and all his outlaws, still you have no right to walk across the corn, and I, George-a-Greene, the Pinner of Wakefield, will drive you off like any other cattle. But if you are brave men and not cowards, come at me one at a time – and I'll trounce you all, and only wish there were twenty such insolent fellows to feel the weight of my staff.'

'Were you as high in deeds,' remarked Scarlet stepping on to the road taking a position of defence, 'as you are in words, you might well qualify as King's Champion. But empty vessels make the loudest sounds, and cowards prattle more than really brave men.'

'Sirrah, dare you to defy me?' shouted George.

'Yes, sirrah, that I dare!' answered Scarlet.

Then they came together striking mighty blows. But the end of it was that George knocked Scarlet a crack on the head and laid him out on the ground.

'Save your blows for a younger man,' exclaimed Little John, and a moment later they too were exchanging blows that rang out like distant thunder across the peaceful evening fields.

But the end of that round was also that Little John felt the pinner's staff on his head more heavily than his senses would stand, and he too joined Scarlet on the ground.

'Come on!' cried Robin, taking John's place. 'Spare me not, and I'll not spare you!'

'Make no doubt of that!' laughed George-a-Greene, 'for I'll be as liberal to you as I was to your friends.'

So they too set to work with their great oaken staffs, and they were so evenly matched that though they fought for an hour, neither got in a decisive blow at the other.

At length they drew apart to rest, and Robin exclaimed, panting for breath:

'Stay, stay, good George! Let us not batter away longer at each other. By my troth, I swear that you are the stoutest champion I ever yet laid hands upon.'

'Softly, softly, good sir,' gasped George. 'By your leave, you lie! You never laid hands on me yet!'

'Well, I admit it,' laughed Robin. 'I have met my match. But come, good George, will you not forsake Wakefield, and go with me? I'll promise you both gain and good fighting if you will but wear my livery of Lincoln green.'

'In God's name, who are you?' asked George, mopping his forehead.

'Why,' answered Robin, 'I am that Robin Hood of whom you spoke – and you have already laid out my two good friends Will Scarlet and Little John.'

'Robin Hood!' cried George. 'Right glad am I to see you! Next to our lord King Richard, you are the man I honour most and have most often longed to meet. Right willingly will I be your man. My time is out as Pinner here in Wakefield and though I will not desert my home, I may well spend some of my days in

Sherwood. And I doubt not that you will find a welcome
also for my dear love Bettris so soon to be my wife?
And if not, the far-famed Maid Marian surely will!'

'Let her answer for herself,' smiled Robin beckoning
to the last member of his party. 'I present Maid Marian
to you!'

Both George and Bettris uttered exclamations of surprise, so perfect was Marian's disguise. But when she
flung back her hood and let the loveliness of her hair
come tumbling all about her face, no one could doubt
that she was far the loveliest lady in all the North
Country, and Bettris, though comely and winsome,
could never compare with her.

But Bettris bore no grudge, and while Robin and
George shook hands and clapped one another on the
back, she went up and knelt before Marian and kissed
her hand.

'Not so,' said Marian gently, 'there is no Lady Marian
in Sherwood but only Maid Marian.' And she raised
Bettris to her feet and embraced and kissed her.

Then they were all happy together, and neither Scarlet nor John bore George any grudge for their broken
heads.

'Come now,' said George, 'you are most welcome.
Come, good Robin Hood, and lovely Maid Marian, and
you two stout fighters, Will Scarlet and Little John –
whose skill with the bow is, I'll warrant, far greater than
mine could ever be. I live but in a humble cottage,
thatched with turf – but I can offer you a feast that you
might not find even in a manor house. I have a side of
beef that has hung in the smoke since Christmas; I have
fresh mutton and veal, I have wafer-cakes in plenty –
and as much ale as any one of you could drink in a
year.'

'And that is a feast all too good for such unbidden

guests as we are,' said Robin. 'But let us in and partake of it. And tomorrow come back with us to Sherwood and taste of our good cheer.'

'Right willingly,' answered George-a-Greene.

'And I say the like,' echoed Bettris. 'That is, if I may come with you dressed even as Marian is, with a sword at my side and a bow on my back.'

'It shall be as you wish,' said George, and Robin nodded agreement. 'But come away now, for dinner waits us – and I long to drink the health of noble Robin Hood!'

CHAPTER SEVENTEEN

A NIGHT ALARM AND A GOLDEN PRIZE

What life is there like to bold Robin Hood?
It is so pleasant a thing:
In merry Sherwood he spends his days
As pleasantly as a king.

ANTHONY MUNDAY: *Metropolis Coronata* (*1615*)

AFTER spending several days at Wakefield with the merry pinner George-a-Greene and his bonny bride Bettris, they all set out once more for Sherwood – Robin Hood, Will Scarlet, and Little John, with Marian dressed also as a forester. George and Bettris came with them, both of them clad now in Lincoln green, and Bettris bubbling over with delight and amusement at being dressed as a man.

Their first day's journey was mainly down the road, and their only moment of danger came when, towards evening, a knight fully armed, with a dozen men at arms behind him, swung round a corner in front of them at a trot and came past before they had any chance of hiding.

The knight did not stop, but his visor was up so that he could see them clearly. He passed without appearing to take any notice, but on looking back Robin saw that he had reined in his horse and was gazing intently after them.

'Walk on as if we had noticed nothing,' said Robin quietly. 'But follow me quickly and quietly into the wood as soon as they are out of sight. I think that was Sir Guy of Gisborne – who is my sworn enemy.'

'And my sworn lover,' added Marian, 'and for that I fear him all the more.'

Once round the corner of the road, Robin led the way quickly into the thick woods, first over flat country, and then along a narrow path which led between rocky and tree-covered hills. Meanwhile the sky became overcast and rain threatened more and more as the evening closed in about them.

'Where are you leading us?' asked George at last.

'To seek shelter for the night,' answered Robin. 'And we shall need it! There are some friends of ours who live near here and are always ready to welcome us – and to help us if any danger threatens, as I fear it may.'

As they wended their way by rough and narrow paths, they met a peasant with a spade over his shoulder.

'Whither go you, my masters?' he asked. 'There be rogues in that direction.'

'Can you show us any direction,' answered Robin, 'in which there are no rogues?'

The peasant grinned, and stood watching them as they threaded their way down the steep side of a valley at the bottom of which a small river dashed and foamed over its rocky bed and glimmered grey and white in the last faint gleams of twilight.

Very soon it was quite dark, and the rising wind, with a whip-lash of rain, foretold a coming storm.

Presently however they saw a light below them, and on Robin winding his horn, an answering note came up to them, and presently they came to a small stone house, little more than a cottage, built on the edge of a steep cliff overhanging the river which swirled through a narrow channel just here and tumbled down a series of low waterfalls.

The door stood invitingly open, and on the threshold was Allin-a-Dale.

'Welcome, welcome, good Robin Hood!' he cried. 'And welcome to your brave followers also! My wife and I are indeed honoured by your company. Come in quickly out of the storm.'

'I fear that we bring danger with us,' said Robin, as they came into the great stone-flagged room which served as kitchen and hall and indeed the whole ground floor of the little house all in one.

And when he had introduced George and Bettris, and made Allin's wife guess who the disguised Marian was, they all sat down on rough benches round the fire to a good meal of broiled meat, with a choice wine to follow it.

Then Robin told Allin of their adventures, and heard all that Allin had to tell him of the difficulty he was having in winning back his wife's lands and house from the clutches of the Bishop of Peterborough.

'These battles of the law,' ended Allin, 'seem as unending as this civil broil between Prince John and the Earl of Chester. I would that King Richard were home again! Then we should have our lands without any further trouble – and a better house than this in which to entertain you.'

Robin sighed. 'If Richard were home again,' he said, 'Marian and I would be man and wife – and, if the King forgives me many things, living once more in my father's house at Locksley, where Sir Guy now dwells. . . . But life in the greenwood is pleasant enough, and I would miss it sorely!'

'Very true,' said Allin, 'but happy though we are in this solitary house, I would like to feel that we were safe.'

Even as he said this, his wife caught him suddenly by the arm and pointed to the one window which was not yet shuttered, and the party following the direction of her hand saw the head of an armed knight with his plumes tossing in the storm on which the light from within the room shone for a second before it disappeared.

In a moment Allin was at the window, swung to the shutters, and dropped the bar into place. As he did so there was a knock at the door, so loud that it must have come from the knuckles of an iron glove.

'Shelter for a poor traveller who has lost his way in the storm!' came a voice from outside.

'Who and what are you?' asked Robin.

'A soldier,' replied the voice, 'an unfortunate follower of Earl Ranulph, flying from the vengeance of Prince John.'

'Are you alone?' said Robin.

'Yes, indeed,' said the voice. 'Pray let me in, kind cottagers – it is a dreadful night. I would not have troubled you but for the storm. I would have slept out in the woods.'

'That I believe,' said Robin. 'You did not expect a storm when you turned into this valley. Do you know that there are rogues this way?'

'I do!' answered the voice.

'So do I!' said Robin.

There was a pause during which Robin, by listening attentively with his ear to the keyhole, caught a faint sound of whispering.

'You are not alone,' declared Robin suddenly. 'Who are your companions?'

'Companions?' exclaimed the voice in surprise. 'I have none, but the wind and rain – and I could do very well without them.'

'The wind and the rain have many voices,' said Robin, 'but I never before heard them say "What shall we do now?"'

There was another pause, and then the voice from without cried in an altogether different tone:

'Look you here, master cottager! If you do not let us in willingly, we will break down the door!'

'Ah-ha!' cried George-a-Greene, who had been listening in silence to all this. ' *We* is it now, you plural rascals? Well, we're ready for you. You thought to rob and murder a poor yeoman and his wife, did you? But instead you come upon a house well garrisoned!'

No reply was made to this, but instead furious blows were dealt to the door which threatened speedily to break it down.

Then Robin, Scarlet, John, and George drew back to the other end of the room, loosened the swords in their sheaths, strung their bows and set each of them an arrow upon the string. Marian without a moment's hesitation took her stand beside Robin and made ready her bow also. But Bettris and Allin's wife armed themselves with spits as long and as sharp as javelins or short throwing spears and took their stands on either side of the doorway. Allin himself stood near his wife with his sword ready in case any of the invaders should break into the house.

At length the door gave with a crash, and a dozen or more armed men were seen in the opening, all with drawn swords in their hands. The instant the door broke the five bows twanged and as many arrows rushed unerringly to their marks, laying three of the invaders dead or sorely wounded on the ground, and disabling two more.

Another man leaping through the doorway fell beneath Allin's sword: Bettris struck at him with her spit, but missing her aim plunged the weapon several inches into the opposite door post where it remained fixed making a new barrier under which all must stoop to enter the house.

The remaining men, however, charged fiercely forward, and one of them wrenched out the spit and hurled

'Guy of Gisborne, I have you at my mercy'

it so mightily at Scarlet and John that, though it turned in the air and struck them only with its side, it stretched both of them on their backs.

Now Robin, Marian, and Allin were fighting with their swords, while George, failing to draw his, snatched up a great wooden cudgel – and felt at once more at home with it than with any other weapon.

Now the fight waged fast and furious, Bettris and Allin's wife joining in as best they could, hurling cooking pots, stools and even articles of china at the most convenient enemy heads. George with two strokes of his cudgel laid two men insensible on the floor, and turned just in time to see Robin's sword shattered to pieces by the iron mace of the knight who commanded the party of attackers. Marian was defending herself valiantly against two swordsmen, and as George charged roaring across the floor to Robin's help, these two turned their attention to him, while Marian leapt forward to meet the knight, parried his blow so dextrously that the sword flew from his hand, and a moment later a well-aimed kettle hurled by Bettris laid him on the floor.

Marian immediately sprang astride him and setting her sword-point to his face, bade him surrender and bid his men cease the combat or she would slay him there and then.

'Mercy, good sir!' gasped the knight, in tones which at once revealed his identity. 'Put down your swords, men: we are fairly beaten.'

'Guy of Gisborne,' said Marian, flinging back her hood so that he could see who had defeated him. 'I have you at my mercy.'

'That I have always been!' gasped the knight, 'and only for love of you have I sought so hard and so often to take you from Robin Hood.'

'How did you find us here?' asked Marian.

'I passed you on the road,' answered Sir Guy, 'and recognized my rival Robin Hood. By the time I had turned and come after you, you were lost in the wood. But a lucky meeting with a peasant at the head of this valley showed me where you were to be found.'

'Sir knight,' said Marian, 'many times you have sought the life of my lord – and of me as well, for I could not live were Robin no more. And do you think me so spiritless as to believe that I could be yours by compulsion? You know well that I would die rather than that – and death is easy to find.'

'Let me strike off his head!' said Robin grimly. 'We have been troubled by this false knight all too long. And now, if he lives, our friends here will be in danger.'

'Not so,' said Marian. 'Sir Guy, you shall swear by the oath you hold most sacred, first that you will seek no vengeance on these good people who shielded us and helped us against you; and second, never more to pursue my lord Robin Hood or me – and on these conditions you shall live.'

'And if you break this oath,' added Robin, 'there is no more mercy for you.'

Then Guy of Gisborne swore what was required by the honour of knighthood and his hope of salvation, and departed into the darkness with all his men, living, dead, or dying.

'We are well rid of an unwelcome guest!' said Robin, when the broken door had been mended as best they could, and the rest of the damage repaired. 'But I am sorry, good friend Allin, and your sweet lady, that this rough and unseemly broil has come to disturb your house.'

'Never trouble about us,' said Allin-a-Dale. 'This has not wiped away even so much as a tenth of our debt to you. And, praise God, none of us are much the worse for

this fray, except for Scarlet and John – and if they drink
enough of my good wine, they can blame their head-
aches on to that!'

'By the Mass!' cried George-a-Greene, 'I love this
life of yours, good Robin, better every hour of it that I
live with you and your merry men. What say you, sweet
Bettris?'

'I would I could wield a sword as well as Maid
Marian,' Bettris answered. 'George, you have failed in
your duties towards me!'

'By not teaching my wife to fight?' laughed George.
'By Our Lady, no court in Christendom would accept
that as a cause of complaint!'

And so the night wore away with laughter and song,
and after they had slept and rested well, the six travellers bade a grateful farewell to Allin-a-Dale and his wife,
and set out once more on their way to Sherwood.

'I hope that no more adventures befall us before we
are safe in our own glades,' said Robin.

But George differed over this, and grew more and
more disappointed as they came further and further
down the road which ran through Sherwood without
meeting any but stray peasants or yeomen.

It was growing again towards evening as they
neared the place for turning off the road into the path
which led towards the secret glade, when suddenly they
heard voices ahead.

'Sssh!' cautioned Robin, and a broad grin overspread
his face. 'I know that voice, it is our fat priest, Friar
Tuck. Come quietly hither behind these bushes, good
George, and I believe that you will see how we gather
our tithes in Sherwood Forest. . . . Yes, the good Friar is
collecting subscriptions for King Richard's ransom!'

The road ran through an overshadowed dell just
there, and peeping over the bushes the travellers saw

Friar Tuck, his mighty quarter-staff in his hand, talking with two trembling priests.

'Benedicite!' boomed Friar Tuck. 'Go not so fast, my brethren! If you cannot spare a piece of silver for the needs of a starving brother, you can at least spare a piece of gold to go towards King Richard's ransom!'

'Alas, alas,' replied the priests. 'We have not so much as a penny piece between us. For this very morning we met with robbers who took from us everything we had.'

'If that be so,' said Friar Tuck, 'then come with me and we will see whether good Robin Hood, the friend of all poor and needy men, cannot lend you some gold out of his store!'

But the two priests showed no desire to follow this suggestion; indeed they were both filled with fear and would have run away there and then if Friar Tuck had not seized each of them by the scruff of the neck and forced them down on to their knees.

'I greatly fear,' he said unctuously, 'that you lack the virtue of truth. And I am resolved to hear your confession before you go hence!'

'Oh spare us, good friar!' wailed the priests. 'Have pity on us!'

'That will I,' quoth Friar Tuck. 'What I do is but for your souls' good. You said just now that you had no money. Therefore let the three of us kneel down here and now and pray that money may come to us!'

There was no help for it, so the priests in trembling voices began to pray for money. And as they prayed they groaned and wrung their hands: but Friar Tuck sang his offices with a fine, full voice, and sang loudest of all when the two priests wept and lamented.

'Now!' said he at length. 'Let us see what money Heaven has sent us in answer to our prayers!'

'No money, no money!' quavered the priests, putting their hands into their pockets.

'Better to search each other's pockets,' said Friar Tuck, and search he did with such good success that more than six hundred pieces of gold were soon laid in a glittering pile on the ground – of which not more than a dozen coins came out of Friar Tuck's pocket.

'Here is a brave show!' cried Friar Tuck when all the pockets were empty. 'Heaven has taught you generosity – even if truth is still denied you. . . . But speak the truth now, or my cudgel shall seek it in your thick heads: whose money is this, and whither were you taking it?'

'Alas!' lamented one of the priests. 'The money was raised by the Abbot of St Mary's, and we were bearing it at his command to good Prince John who is now at Ashby-de-la-Zouche not far south from here.'

'Then indeed,' cried Friar Tuck happily, 'it could be put to no better use than to complete the ransom which shall set free our dear King Richard to come home into this unhappy country and punish the wickedness and cruelty of Prince John and his evil followers. Here I give you one piece of gold each: that will take you to Ashby. And if Prince John does not reward you handsomely for using his money in so good a cause – why, you must sell your horses or beg your way back to York! Now, get you gone speedily, and say that Robin Hood is forwarding the ransom money for his King's return.'

The two frightened priests, still weeping and lamenting, clambered upon their horses which stood waiting at a little distance, and went galloping away in a cloud of dust, while Friar Tuck stood by his pile of gold and bellowed with laughter.

'Stand, base Friar!' shouted Robin suddenly in a feigned voice. 'Down on your knees, or I send an arrow into your heart! There are six of us here, and we will have no mercy unless you render up your gold!'

Down on his knees in the dust went Friar Tuck, the laughter cut short suddenly. But, as he heard the six coming up behind him, he leapt to his feet, whirled up his staff and rushed upon them roaring:

'Robin Hood for ever!'

'Have a care with that great twig of yours!' laughed Robin. 'If you drop that on my head it will be Robin Hood for his everlasting rest!'

'Robin! Good Robin! And John and Scarlet!' cried the Friar. 'And gentle Maid Marian too! How filled with joy I am to see you!... Look you here what I have collected, a golden prize for you!'

'And look what I bring with me,' answered Robin. 'Brave George-a-Greene the Pinner of Wakefield, who now is one of us, and with him his bride the lovely Bettris. Make them welcome, good Friar!'

'Welcome they are, by the Mass!' boomed Friar Tuck. 'And welcome are you back to Sherwood. Oh, there will be feasting and drinking tonight. Come away quickly, I am like to faint with hunger and thirst at the very idea!'

And away they went, arm in arm through the forest, Friar Tuck carrying his golden prize, and singing right lustily:

> Robin and Marian, Scarlet and Little John,
> Drink to them one by one, drink as ye sing:
> Robin and Marian, Scarlet and Little John,
> Echo to echo through Sherwood shall fling:
> Robin and Marian, Scarlet and Little John,
> Long with their glory old Sherwood shall ring!

CHAPTER EIGHTEEN

THE WITCH OF PAPLEWICK

> *His scene is Sherwood, and his play a Tale*
> *Of Robin Hood's inviting from the vale*
> *Of Belvoir all the shepherds to a feast*
> *Where by the casual absence of one guest*
> *The mirth is troubled much. . . .*
>
> BEN JONSON: *The Sad Shepherd* (1640)

ONE of the strangest adventures that ever befell Robin
Hood and his company chanced at a time when they
had left the deeper glades of Sherwood for the open
parkland and the green downs where the shepherds and
shepherdesses of Paplewick lived their simple, carefree
life far from all wars and discords.

On a sweet summer's day Robin Hood decided to
hold a feast at which to entertain all the shepherds and
shepherdesses, besides his own merry men. Marian with
Scarlet and several others went forth to kill the deer,
while Robin greeted each of his guests. But one guest
was missing, the shepherd Eglamour.

'Where is he, who was wont to sing such sweet songs?'
asked Robin, and the shepherd Lionel replied:

'Alas, good Robin, Eglamour has lost his love, the
beauteous Earine, drowned only a few days since in passing over the river Trent. Her body was never recovered,
and Eglamour will not believe that she is dead, but
seeks her still by wood and wold, calling her name until
I think the very birds weep for him.'

'That is a sadness hard to be comforted,' said Robin.
'Yet go you in search of him, friend Lionel, and let

Much go with you also. Seek if you may find him and
bring him to our feast.'

Scarcely had they set out in search of Eglamour, when
a horn sounded near by, and Marian returned walking
proudly in advance while Scarlet and the rest followed
behind with the deer cut up and ready to cook.

'My Marian!' cried Robin.

'Robin, my love!' she answered. 'Oh, now my day's
happiness is complete! I rose early, early before the sun,
and such fine sport we had seeking the deer. Then one
shot brought him down, a long shot, and my arrow in his
heart. And now to find you waiting with all our friends!'

'We did but wait for you,' said Robin. 'This is a day
of joy indeed.'

'Only one shadow fell upon us,' said Marian. 'When
we had killed the deer and cut it up, a raven sat upon
the tree over our heads and croaked dismally.'

'It was but waiting for its share!' laughed Robin.
'They are wise birds and know that it is ever the huntsman's custom, when he cleaves the brisket bone to set
aside the spoon of it with the gristle that grows there –
which indeed is often called the Raven's Bone.'

'I know,' said Marian, 'but the shepherd Karolin
who was with us swore that it was no ordinary raven,
but Mother Maudlin the Witch of Paplewick who, it is
said, can take any form she will. Karolin met Maudlin
in the dawning as he was rousing the deer for us – and
says she cursed him, promising that ill things would
this day befall any who ate of the deer at Robin Hood's
feast!'

Marian said this half laughing, and yet half in fear,
for indeed at that time all men believed in witchcraft –
and doubtless that was why there were then still witches
to be found who were indeed in touch with the darker
powers of evil.

While Marian went to wash in the stream nearby, Robin turned to Karolin the shepherd and asked him about Mother Maudlin.

'She is indeed a witch,' answered Karolin. 'Some call her just a wise woman, but most of us know better. And I know for sure that she is an arrant witch, and a shape-shifter at that.'

'How are you so certain?' asked Robin.

'Why, I saw her but a moment since,' answered Karolin. 'Down by the stream she had kindled a little fire and there was broiling the very bone we threw to the raven at the kill!'

During the pause which followed his statement, Marian came hastening back to them. But now all the joy and gaiety had died out of her face, and her eyes seemed cold and hard.

'How now, sweet Marian?' began Robin. 'Shall we to the feast?'

'Feast?' cried Marian, her voice growing shrill with anger. 'What feast?'

'Why, Marian, how strange you look,' said Robin. 'Say, has anything chanced to cause you fear or pain?'

'Oh, I am well!' snapped Marian. 'I am better than ever I was.'

'Then let us call our friends to the feast,' repeated Robin, still looking at her with a troubled expression.

'Friends!' cried Marian. 'They shall not feast on this venison! It is too good for such coarse, rustic mouths that cannot open to thank for it. A starved sheep's carcase would suit them better. ... Scarlet, take up the venison – swiftly now! Carry it to Mother Maudlin, the wise woman whom you call a witch, tell her I sent it: she at least will be grateful and return me her kind thanks.'

'Marian! Can this be true!' gasped Robin. 'Friends,

tell me that I am but dreaming, that I am not Robin Hood nor this my Marian?'

'You are Robin Hood right enough,' snapped Marian. 'You it is who spy on everything I do, and follow me everywhere with your jealousy and oppression. . . . I'll give the venison to whom I please. I shot the deer, and it is mine to dispose of. And you shall not call my kind friend Maudlin a witch. . . . Go and swill ale with these vulgar shepherds and their girls: I can bear your company no more today!'

And with that she strode away into the wood leaving them all speechless.

'I fear she is stricken with some illness,' said Robin at last. 'Never has she been like this before . . . I will go seek her. . . . But do her bidding, Scarlet, and take the venison to Mother Maudlin. . . . Friends, forgive me. This has spoilt all the joy of our merrymaking: but I trust that all may yet be set right.'

Then Robin went off into the wood, and presently he found Marian sitting by the stream with a shepherdess called Amie who was telling her all the sad tale of Eglamour and the lost Earine.

'Oh, my love!' cried Marian so soon as she saw Robin. 'Forgive me for staying so long away from you.' And she ran towards Robin with her arms outstretched.

But Robin said sternly: 'And am I now your love, and no longer a spy who follows you everywhere with my jealousy and oppression?'

'Spy? Jealousy?' gasped Marian. 'Oh, Robin, what do you mean?'

'Did you not leave our guests declaring that a starved sheep's carcase was all they were fit for, and send Will Scarlet to carry the venison to Mother Maudlin?'

'I, to Mother Maudlin?' gasped Marian. 'Does Scarlet say that?'

'You cannot deny it,' said Robin, 'for here is Lionel who heard it all – and here comes Scarlet himself!'

'Alas!' cried Marian, her eyes filling with tears. 'This is some cruel jest you are practising on me. I never said any of these things, nor sent the venison to Mother Maudlin. I came here to the stream to wash, and would have returned at once had I not found Amie and stayed to hear of the sad loss of Earine.'

By this time Scarlet had joined them.

'I have done your bidding,' he said, 'and taken the venison to Mother Maudlin's.'

'Alas!' cried Marian again. 'You are all in league against me! I never gave you any such command. I have been here all the time with Amie, ever since I left you, just after Lionel had told you of the raven and Mother Maudlin.'

'The raven and the witch!' exclaimed Scarlet. 'By Our Lady, there is something strange in all this! Is it your will, good Lady Marian, that I bring back the venison?'

'It is indeed,' answered Marian, and away went Scarlet at full speed.

'Good Robin Hood,' said Amie. 'I swear before God that Maid Marian has been here with me for at least the half of an hour – and when she came it was with hands defiled from the deer which she purposed but to wash in the stream.'

'This is strange,' began Robin. 'Yet how can our senses so have been deceived?'

'Look you!' interrupted Lionel suddenly, 'here comes Mother Maudlin herself, and Little John is with her.'

Sure enough, there was the old woman, who was supposed to be a witch, a bent form with long grey locks and fierce rather cruel eyes, hobbling swiftly along beside the gigantic person of her guide.

'Good master,' called Little John as soon as they were

near enough. 'Here is Mother Maudlin who would speak with you. She says that she comes in gratitude for some gift sent her by Maid Marian.'

'Aye, kind hearts!' cried Maudlin shrilly. 'Sent me a stag, she did, a whole stag for poor old Maudlin – the fattest deer that ever I set eyes on. So fairly hunted, and at such a time too, when all your friends went hungry for the gift of it!'

'It is true, then,' said Robin in a low voice.

'Oh, such a bounty to a poor old woman!' continued Maudlin. 'Oh, I shall go crazy with the joy of it!'

'Surely, good mother,' said Marian, 'there is some mistake. This deer was indeed the meat intended to feast our dear friends the shepherds and shepherdesses of Paplewick – for whom the best stag in all Sherwood Forest could not be too good. Bethink you, my foresters were much mistaken to bear it all away to you; or else some madness had come upon me, if I indeed gave such an order. So you will not take it, dear Mother Maudlin, I dare swear, if we intreat you, now that you know who are our guests. Remember that red deer is still the choicest dish at any forest feast.'

'But I know your charity, dear lady,' whined Maudlin. 'And you can well spare it. . . . And I cannot return it now, for already I have divided it all among my poor neighbours in and around Paplewick.'

'I gave it not!' cried Marian, wringing her hands. 'Either it was stolen, or else there has been witchcraft here!'

Just at that moment Will Scarlet came running swiftly and saluted Robin Hood.

'Good master,' he said. 'The deer is back once more in your kitchen. I found it all together where Mother Maudlin had laid it away. But now our fellow Reynolde is making it ready to cook.'

'Do you give a thing, and then take it back again?'
cried Maudlin.

'No, Maudlin,' replied Marian, her eyes flashing.
'We took it not. For you had it no longer, but had
given it away among your neighbours! I have done no
wrong.'

Then Maudlin waved her hands in the air and
shrieked curses on their feast and especially on Reynolde
the cook.

> *The spit stand still and no joints turn*
> *Before the fire, but let it burn*
> *Both sides and haunches till the whole*
> *Converted be into one coal!*
> *The stinking dropsy enter in*
> *Your filthy cook and swell his skin,*
> *The pain we call the gout begin*
> *To prick and itch from toe to shin,*
> *And cramp the cook in every limb —*
> *Before you dine, all this on him!*

And away she hobbled, still cursing freely, and chanting her wicked rhymes in a shrill voice.

'By the Mass,' exclaimed Robin, crossing himself.
'She is a witch indeed. I believe she can take any shape,
as Lionel hinted. And if I could but see her once more in
Marian's form, which I almost believe she wore a little
while since, I would know for certain how we have been
abused and cheated. . . . Sweet Marian, forgive me for
doubting you! With this kiss I call you all to witness my
penance.'

Just at this moment Friar Tuck came puffing up, followed by several others of Robin's men.

'Here's a to-do!' gasped the Friar. 'Poor Reynolde
the cook is taken with the gout or cramp all of a sudden!
He is all ridden with aches and pains, he cannot stand,

Witches lived in deep, dark caves, by ruined churchyards,
among gaping graves

he cannot stir hand or foot and, worse of all, he cannot
cook!'

'Then indeed he is bewitched!' cried Lionel the shepherd. 'And Mother Maudlin has done it even now with
charms and her curses!'

'What's to be done?' asked Robin.

'She must be restrained!' cried Lionel, 'otherwise
she'll do a worse mischief. She'll have some charm upon
her, some magic belt or locket or talisman.'

'All right,' exclaimed Robin. 'Some of you – Little
John, George-a-Greene, Scarlet – go with Lionel in
search of her. You, good Friar and Much, go back and
cook our dinner, it were a pity to spoil it!'

'By the Mass, that were the greatest pity of all!' cried
Friar Tuck. 'Come, Much – let us make haste to save
our dinner!'

So they set off in several directions, Lionel telling
John and the rest with many ghastly details how witches
always lived in deep, dark caves by ruined churchyards
and among gaping graves, making hideous brews out of
sad mandrake, deadly nightshade, stupifying hemlock,
and poisonous adders' tongues.

Robin and Marian stayed behind with Amie the
shepherdess, for she assured them that Eglamour the sad
shepherd was certain to pass that way, still lamenting
for his lost love, and then they might stop and comfort
him.

Sure enough Eglamour came presently walking like a
shadow among the tall ferns and grasses, and singing of
his lost Earine:

> *Here was she wont to go! and here! and here!*
> *Just where those daisies, pinks and violets grow;*
> *The world might find the Spring by following her,*
> *For other print her airy steps ne'er left.*

Her treading would not bend a blade of grass,
Or shake the downy blow-ball from his stalk!
But like the soft west wind she shot along,
And where she went, the flowers took thickest root,
As she had sowed them with her odorous foot.

'Good shepherd,' said Robin Hood kindly, as Eglamour paused beside them, his voice dying away in sobs.
'Good shepherd, be comforted. Such grief I know can
find no cure save only time: but you must fight against
it, and we will help you – '

'She is drowned!' cried Eglamour wildly. 'Drowned
in the Trent! Maybe she fled away from some vile man
– but she, as chaste as was her name, Earine – died in
the cold stream, my lovely maid. And now her sweet
soul hovers here in the air above us – oh, Earine, Earine!
I come!'

And on a sudden he fled away into the wood, yet not
so suddenly but that both Robin and Marian could dis-
tinctly see the figure of a girl flitting away in front of
him.

'By Our Lady,' said Robin. 'Yonder indeed *is* Earine
– or her ghost.'

'Or . . . Robin, do you think Maudlin could be up to
more of her tricks?' gasped Marian.

'I'll follow!' shouted Robin. 'Stay you here with
Amie!' And away he went over the springy turf and
among the trees.

Very soon he lost sight of Eglamour, but still every
now and then he could see the slim form that looked like
Earine speeding on ahead of him.

At last he came among dark rocks and trees blasted
by lightning, where for a while he was quite lost, until
at length he heard shouts and a horn which he recognized as Little John's, and following the sounds came

suddenly upon a dark house or hovel built against the
cliff side and above a deep pool in the rocks into which a
waterfall thundered, and where the water swirled round
as if in a giant's cauldron.

Outside the house stood Little John and Eglamour,
and in the doorway was Marian. Robin paused in
amazement, and watched unseen.

'You are mistaken, good John, greatly mistaken,'
Marian was saying. 'They say that Maudlin is a witch
but that is false. It is only that she is far wiser than other
women, and knows the cure for many sicknesses and
wounds. Therefore leave her in peace, good John; return
to Robin and tell him what I say, and beg him as he
loves me not to pursue her further – for she is my dear
friend.'

'This may be true, Lady Marian,' said Little John
uncertainly, 'but Robin must decide that for himself.
Here I bide until he comes!' And with that he blew
another call on his horn.

Then Robin stepped out into view.

'You run well, Marian!' he began. 'Faster than I do.
and yet – '

But he had no time for more, for Marian, as soon as
she saw him, uttered a scream of terror and turning
struggled to open the door of the hovel.

Robin sprang forward, and as he did so saw that
about her waist she wore a strange girdle curiously
embroidered with mystic signs. . . . He had seen it before
. . . But not round Marian's waist. . . . Surely Mother
Maudlin wore just such a girdle?

Robin seized the girdle just as the door flew open. It
broke in his hand, remaining there as Marian disappeared into the darkness within.

A moment later Maudlin rushed out:

'Help! Murder! Help!' she screamed. 'You will not

rob me, outlaw? Wicked thief, restore my girdle that you have broken!'

'Was this some charmed circle,' said Robin grimly, as he looked at the broken girdle in his hand, 'was this the cause of our deceptions? ... Look you, Mother Maudlin, there is no place for such as you in Sherwood Forest, nor in Paplewick, nor anywhere among the haunts of good men and honest women. Now get you gone from here. There goes your charm!' and as he spoke he flung the broken girdle far out into the seething pool beneath the waterfall.

'Now go!' he commanded. 'If you are visible five minutes from now, my men shall hunt you like a wolf. And if ever they see you again they have my command to shoot you as they would a wolf – and as I shall shoot you if ever you cross my path again.'

Then Mother Maudlin turned and fled away swiftly, without a word, and was never more seen at Paplewick, nor anywhere in Sherwood Forest.

But Robin and Little John and Eglamour entered the hovel, and there they found Earine alive and well, but gagged and bound so that she could neither move nor cry out.

When they had released her and Eglamour, his wits quite restored at the sight of his beloved, had carried her away into the forest, Robin and John set fire to that evil dwelling, and stood by until only smouldering ashes remained to show where the witch of Paplewick had lived.

Then they returned in joy and triumph to the feast, where Marian and Amie were waiting for them, and Friar Tuck was just serving up the savoury joints of venison.

There was wild rejoicing over the recovery of Earine, and Friar Tuck swore that after dinner he would solemnize two marriages – not only Lionel and Amie, but Eglamour and Earine as well.

'But now to dinner!' he cried, 'that comes before all!' And with that he sang,

> *Now to the feast, the greenwood feast,*
> *With happy heart each rural guest!*
> *Sound, bugles, sound! each nymph and swain*
> *Join in the cheerful choral strain;*
> *And nimbly trip it through the wood*
> *To the famed feast of Robin Hood!*

CHAPTER NINETEEN

THE LAST OF GUY OF GISBORNE

Now take thou golde and fee!
Sir Guy, well cume mote thou bee!
Golde and fee wylle I none,
But yon outlawe alone.

ANON: *Folk Play of Robin Hood (before 1476)*

IT was a glorious Spring morning, the new leaves were fully opened, the greensward all fresh and daisy-clad, and the birds sang merrily in every tree and bush.

Loudest of all sang the thrush who sat upon a spray of white hawthorn, so loud that at length he wakened Robin Hood who slept in the mouth of his cave nearby in the secret glade in Sherwood Forest.

'Now, by my faith!' cried Robin as he sat up, to find his men already moving about the glade, preparing breakfast. 'I had a strange dream that kept me sleeping. I dreamed of two strong foresters who fought with me. And I dreamed that they overcame me and bound me. Then they beat me and took my bow away from me. . . . I trust that this dream bodes no evil to me or to any of us this day.'

'Dreams are light things,' said Little John. 'They come like the wind that blows over the hill – however loud it may be in the night, in the morning there may be no wind at all.'

'Nevertheless,' said Robin, 'we know that the Sheriff of Nottingham has been gathering men and sending spies through the forest this month past. He intends something against us, depend upon it.'

'And we are ready for him,' answered Little John. 'Every path leading towards this glade is prepared, and men are on watch night and day.'

'Then let them all be ready this day,' said Robin, 'and especially on guard. But John, you and I will go out into the greenwood – to see whether we chance upon the two men of my dream.'

Robin Hood and Little John set out accordingly, and they had not gone half a mile when they saw a man dressed as a forester, with his hood rather over his face, leaning against a tree with a bow in his hand. By his side hung sword and dagger, and his jerkin was of horsehide.

'Stand you here, good master,' said Little John, 'under this shadowy tree. And I will go and speak with yonder strong forester and see if he intends us any harm.'

But Robin answered rather more sharply than usual, perhaps still troubled by his dream or over anxious on account of the Sheriff's expected attack:

'I am not accustomed to let my men go first while I follow after them into danger. You put yourself forward too much, John – and I've half a mind to cut me a staff and give you a good beating – to show that I can still strike a shrewd blow or two.'

Little John was also violent of temper, but he was accustomed to these occasional outbursts from Robin.

'Then I'll leave you to try whether dreams speak true,' he said. 'I'll go along the Nottingham road and see if all is quiet there.'

Off went Little John accordingly, and was soon whistling happily as he traced the forest paths and came out onto the grassy Nottingham road.

But here he was brought up suddenly with no further desire to whistle. For in the grass on the roadside two men lay dead with arrows in their hearts, and it needed only a glance to tell John that both of them were fellow outlaws and members of Robin's band. And even while he stood by them he heard shouts, and Will Scarlet came down the road, running for his life, and behind him a whole troop of the Sheriff's men and with them several of Sir Guy's men at arms, and two or three verderers.

One verderer, William Trent, whom John knew well and had once thrashed at quarter-staff stepped up onto a log and loosed his arrow, and Will Scarlet pitched forward onto his face.

'It were better for you, William Trent, that your hand had been smitten off at the wrist ere ever you fired that shot!' cried Little John, and as he spoke his bow twanged, and Will Scarlet's slayer lay dead in the high road. And so mightily had Little John drawn his bow in his grief and rage that the arrow passed clean through William Trent and slew another man who stood behind him. But the very fury of the shot was Little John's undoing, for the bow broke into several pieces, and before he could draw his sword the Sheriff's men were upon him and he was bound hand and foot.

The Sheriff rode up and surveyed Little John from head to foot.

'Here,' he said exultantly, 'we have one of the worst rascals of them all! Fellow, you shall be drawn at a rope's end by down and dale back to Nottingham, and hanged on the castle hill!'

'But, if God wills it otherwise,' answered Little John, 'you may yet be cheated of your purpose.'

'There will be no escape this time,' said the Sheriff with a grim smile. 'For what can your wretched gang of outlaws do against the seven score men who are out this day to rid Sherwood Forest of the whole pack of you?'

'Now Heaven protect my good master Robin Hood,' said Little John, and he blamed himself sorely for leaving him alone merely because of a hasty word.

Meanwhile Robin had gone forward to speak with the solitary forester, who stood waiting for him beneath the tree.

'Good morrow, good fellow,' said Robin courteously. 'By the fine bow you carry in your hand, I take it that you are an archer, and a good one too.'

'That am I,' answered the stranger with a strong west country accent. 'And a stranger in these parts who cannot find his way through these woods.'

'Come with me then,' said Robin, 'and I will guide you on your way. What do you here, and where do you wish to go?'

'I seek a man they call Robin Hood,' said the stranger, 'for fain would I serve him and be one of his company.'

'That is easily accomplished,' Robin assured him. 'Come with me and I will lead you to where he dwells.'

They strode through the wood for some time, the stranger always keeping his head down as if in deep thought. More than once he showed signs of dropping behind, but Robin was always ready to slacken his pace and apologize for his speed.

Presently the stranger said:

'Good sir, let us pause awhile in this glade and rest.'

'Right willingly,' answered Robin. 'But while we are here, let us see how good a marksman you are.'

'That is well thought of,' said the stranger eagerly, and he strung his bow and set an arrow on the string.

'At what shall we shoot?' asked Robin. 'The stump over yonder must be two hundred yards and more, and

I see a white patch of lichen on it which will make a fine bull's eye.'

'Fie!' cried the stranger scornfully. 'Is that all you of Sherwood can do? Why, in Pendle Forest we would think scorn of so easy a mark.'

Robin flushed at this.

'I'll set you a Sherwood mark,' he said angrily, 'that few men in the world can hit even at fifty yards!'

With that he flung down his bow and quiver, and strode down the glade, pausing to cut a slim hazel wand which he began to peel with his hunting knife.

'Robin Hood!' called the stranger when he had gone a dozen yards or so – and now his voice had changed, and there was no longer any trace of an accent in it. But Robin spun round at the sound of the voice, for he recognized it as that of Guy of Gisborne, even if the stranger had not thrown off his hood.

'This is the last round,' said Guy grimly, and very slowly and deliberately he drew back the string of his bow, the point of his arrow in a line with Robin's heart.

'Coward as well as forsworn knight and false traitor,' said Robin quietly. 'Will you not even meet me fairly, man to man and sword to sword? There is no shame in that: I am gently born as yourself, you know well: but to shoot an unarmed man is shame indeed – and damnation to follow.'

Sir Guy flushed a little at Robin's words, for seldom indeed can those who are nobly born crush out the last flicker of the honour which is their birth-portion. But he only said:

'When Robert of Locksley became Robin Hood of Sherwood he was cast out beyond the law of man and beyond the pale of honour. In a little while I shall wind my horn and thereby the Sheriff shall know that Robin Hood is dead: and by then the half of your followers will be dead or captive also. But if you like to yield yourself prisoner to me now, I can promise you a gallows in Nottingham.'

'Why then,' said Robin. 'I choose an arrow in Sherwood – if you can plant one in my heart!'

As he spoke he stooped slightly, and then with a sudden movement flung the knife which he still held in his hand and flung himself forward flat on the ground with the same movement.

The knife flashed through the air as Guy's bow twanged: the arrow flew above Robin's head and as Guy raised his arm to ward off the knife its flashing blade bit deep into his bow, and glanced off, wounding him slightly in the cheek as it passed.

A moment later Robin was on his feet again, his sword drawn in his hand, and charged down upon Guy, who flung aside his useless bow and also drew his sword.

'This is indeed the last round,' cried Robin. 'But now the combat is even – and may God defend the right!'

Then they came together, lashing and smiting with their swords until the sparks flew.

It was not a long combat. Once Guy's sword grazed Robin's neck, but the next instant Robin swung his blade with a shout and smote Guy in the side. But the sword rebounded, and Guy did but stagger a little.

'Chain armour!' cried Robin, and he stepped back hastily to avoid Guy's return blow – and tripped over a tree root.

'Dear Mary, Mother of God, intercede for me now!' prayed Robin, and he warded off the stab, which Guy aimed at his body with such good effect that Guy stumbled and drove his sword into the ground.

That moment saved Robin, and the next he whirled up his sword and smote Guy a backhanded blow from beneath which clove the bone of his forehead. Then Sir

Guy of Gisborne reeled back, his sword fell from his hand, and with one terrible cry he fell to the ground and died.

Robin stood panting for a little while, looking on the dead body of his enemy. Then he said grimly:

'There lies a false and dishonoured man, but in his death he may yet do good.' With that he smote off Guy's head, took off his own hood and wrapped it in it. Then he put on Guy's horse-skin jerkin and Guy's large hood. Finally he took the bugle-horn out of Guy's pouch and wound it long and loud.

An answer came directly from no very great distance, and Robin set off at once towards the sound, pausing only to sling his own bow and arrows over his shoulder.

The Sheriff and the main body of his men were still marching into the depths of the forest, being joined every now and then by stray parties bringing with them news of guards posted to prevent the outlaws escaping.

When the sound of the horn came echoing through the trees the Sheriff nearly fell off his horse with delight.

'A mort! A mort!' he cried. 'Hearken to that! Sir Guy of Gisborne's horn! That means he has killed Robin Hood – the best tidings that ever I heard!' And with that he lugged out his own bugle horn and blew an answering call.

Very soon Robin appeared walking quickly through the forest, carrying the head hanging in the blood-stained hood.

'Yonder he comes!' cried the excited Sheriff. 'I know him by his jerkin of horse-hide put on to disguise the chain mail underneath. Come hither, come hither good Sir Guy and ask of me any reward you will!'

'I ask none,' said Robin, keeping his face as much in shadow as possible, and imitating Sir Guy's voice, 'for I have ever hated this man whose head I bring to you here – and the feud between us could be ended by death alone. But if you would do ought to pleasure me, I ask but this: As I have slain the master, give me the man to slay as and when I will!'

And turning quickly, Robin pointed to Little John, who now lay bound upon the ground with several others of the outlaws.

'A mad choice when gold might have been yours for the asking!' said the Sheriff; 'but such as it is, I give it to you freely. There lies the fellow they call Little John: he is yours to kill.'

When Little John heard this, he thought that he was dreaming – and still more so when Robin knelt down beside him, knife in hand, and began to cut his bonds, whispering:

'It is I, Robin Hood! When you are loose, wait until I call out, then take my bow and arrows which I shall leave on the grass beside you, and we will at least sell our lives more dearly than the Sheriff dreams of.'

When he had loosed Little John, Robin moved quickly to the next prisoner, and he had cut the bonds of two other members of his band before the Sheriff realized what he was doing.

'No, no, Sir Guy!' he cried. 'I granted you one life, not three!'

'But I'll take another!' shouted Robin, and throwing off Sir Guy's hood, he leapt upon the nearest of the Sheriff's foresters, and in a moment had laid him dead on the ground and seized his bow, arrows, and sword.

'To me, Little John!' he cried, and straightway Little John sprang to his feet an arrow on the string, and stood beside him.

'It is Robin Hood – or the devil!' shrieked the Sheriff. 'Cut him down!' And he tumbled backwards off his horse just in time to avoid an arrow which caught the man behind him in the throat.

Then Robin and John shot fast and well, but the odds were too great, and presently they were forced to drop their bows and defend themselves with their swords.

Once Robin paused in the fight, and at infinite risk drew out his own horn and sounded a piercing call on it. Then he fought on, and the two other outlaws whom he had loosed snatched up swords from beside the men who had fallen to their arrows, and fought desperately too.

Valiantly though they fought, they would have been overwhelmed by sheer numbers before help could arrive had it not been for a sudden unexpected interruption.

A knight clad from head to foot in black armour and riding a great black horse, came riding up the road. The moment he saw the throng of men he snapped his visor shut – and rode closer.

Then he suddenly unslung a mighty axe which hung at his saddle-bow and spurred his horse into the centre of the Sheriff's men, shouting in a great voice:

'What, so many against so few? Back, you damned wolves! I cannot see four men borne down by such a host! Charge, foresters! St George for merry England!'

At this unexpected attack many of the Sheriff's men broke and fled – and the first of all to set the example was the Sheriff himself, who had remounted his horse and now set spurs to it and got back to Nottingham, safe except for an arrow which Little John managed to plant in his backside as he disappeared round the corner out of sight.

The Black Knight paused only for a moment to shout: 'Stay, you base curs! Or I'll beat you back to your kennel!' Then he thundered down the road after the Sheriff and those of his men who were mounted, and

The Sheriff's men broke and fled, first of all the Sheriff himself, remounted on his horse disappeared from view. But now Robin's men, brought by the bugle-call, came pouring in from every side, and the rest of the Sheriff's great company flung down their arms and either surrendered or ran for their lives.

'Where is Will Scarlet?' asked Robin suddenly.

'I came too late to save him,' answered Little John sadly. 'But I slew the man, William Trent, who killed him, before they took me.'

Then Robin's brow became very dark. 'Trent,' he said, 'the head verderer of the Forest? . . . Let no verderer live this day. As for the Sheriff's men, they are poor serfs for the most part, forced to serve him. Strip all of them to their shirts, tie their hands behind them, hang halters round their necks and let them trudge barefoot back to Nottingham. Take command here, Little John: I follow the verderers.'

Away went Robin, running swiftly through the Forest where he knew every path and all the shortest cuts, until he came out at the top of the hillside leading down towards Nottingham. The road was below him, and on it were several of the Sheriff's men running for their lives. Robin let these pass, but presently when a troop of verderers or forest rangers in their Kendal green coats came into view, he shouted in a mighty voice:

'Verderers of Sherwood! I exact vengeance from you alone, for you have this day slain my friend Will Scarlet. Run now to Nottingham – the gate is but a mile away! He who passes the gate may live: but so long as you are on the road, I shoot, and Robin Hood's arrows do not miss!'

Then the fifteen verderers turned and shot at Robin as he stood on the hillside above them. But so great was their fear that not one of their arrows struck him. Then they threw down their bows and ran for their lives.

Robin drew fifteen arrows from his quiver and set

them in the grass before him. Then he set the first to his
bow, drew, and loosed it at the last of the verderers who
was already many hundred yards away from him.

'One!' he shouted as the arrow sped and the man
pitched forward on the road.

'Two!' and the next man lay dead also.

And so he drew and loosed arrow after arrow, and so
great was his grief and his rage at the death of Will
Scarlet that each of those fifteen arrows was the death
of a man – though the last man to fall was within a hundred yards of the gate of Nottingham. Yes, though the
distance between them was nearly a mile, the last arrow
came humming down wind and took the man in the
back of the neck – the longest shot that ever a man fired
with a long-bow.

Afterwards the people of Nottingham, who had seen
Robin's feat of archery, came out in fear and trembling
and took up the fifteen bodies. They buried them side by
side in the yard of St Michael's church at Fox Lane by
Nottingham; and there, less than two hundred years
ago, the skeletons of six of them were found lying side by
side, and buried again, to bear witness to Robin Hood's
amazing bowmanship.

CHAPTER TWENTY

THE SILVER BUGLE AND THE BLACK KNIGHT

High deeds achieved of knightly fame,
From Palestine the champion came;
The cross upon his shoulders borne,
Battle and blast had dimmed and torn.
Each dint upon his battered shield
Was token of a foughten field.

SIR WALTER SCOTT: *Ivanhoe* (1820)

THE news of a shooting-match would draw Robin Hood out of Sherwood, however great the danger, and not many days after the death of Will Scarlet and the rout of the Sheriff and his men, Robin set forth for Ashby-de-la-Zouche in Leicestershire.

A great tournament was being held there by Prince John – but the danger to Robin was not so great as when he had won the Silver Arrow at Delamere. For Prince John, though his power had increased greatly, was by no means accepted as King of England. There were rumours that Richard was free again from his Austrian captivity – rumours even that he was in England. John believed none of these, but his policy was to please as many of his future subjects as possible: the tournament was for Saxons as well as Normans, and Robin knew that whatever might happen in secret, John would never attempt to take him in the midst of a crowd such as was gathered at Ashby-de-la-Zouche.

The main features of the Tournament were of course for the knights. On the first day there was jousting with lances, the knights riding together at full tilt, in complete armour, striving to knock each other from their horses. The winner in this was an unknown knight, and on the next day he headed one side in the 'mock battle' – which was apt to become very real indeed. The other side was headed by Sir Brian de Bois-Guilbert who had come second in the jousting, and on his side were several other Norman barons well known for their cruelty and oppression – and sworn followers of Prince John.

All that morning the battle raged, and it would have gone ill with the Unknown Knight had not his party been joined by the same Black Knight who had come so mysteriously to Robin's aid in Sherwood not many days before. The Black Knight took little part in the combat until his party showed signs of suffering defeat: then his sudden fury in fight and the mighty strength of his blows won the day for the unknown knight – who turned out to be a certain Sir Wilfred of Ivanhoe, one of King Richard's most faithful friends, but of Saxon descent. Sir Wilfred was wounded in the combat, and fainted just as the crown of victory was being placed on his head by the Lady Rowena whom he had chosen Queen of the Lists after his triumph on the previous day.

When he had been carried away to be tended, Prince John declared that the time had come for the archery contest.

More than thirty yeomen at first presented themselves, but when they recognized Robin Hood among those who were contesting for the prize, nearly three-quarters of them withdrew.

'Who is that fellow?' asked Prince John, who was sitting high up on the stand among the lords and ladies who were there to watch the Tournament.

'They call him Locksley,' answered the Provost of the Lists.

'Locksley!' John started at the name, and leaning down scanned the archer more closely. 'I thought so!' he said between his teeth.

At this moment Robin looked up and their eyes met. Prince John made a movement as if to order Robin's arrest, but one of his councillors restrained him quickly.

'Hark ye, Locksley – or whatever you choose to call yourself,' said Prince John, when he had recovered his temper a little.

Robin turned and bowed respectfully to Prince John. 'What would your Highness with me?' he asked.

'I know you, Robert Fitzooth –' began the Prince, spitting between his teeth with suppressed rage.

'Locksley is my name, if it please your Highness,' interrupted Robin politely.

'It does not please me!' spluttered Prince John. 'But nevertheless you are safe here – as doubtless you realized before you trusted yourself in my presence.'

Robin returned no answer to this, and the shooting began. One by one the archers stepped forward, and each discharged two arrows of which some failed even to hit the distant target, and only two landed in the gold. Both of these were shot by a certain Hubert, head verderer in the royal forest of Needwood.

'Now, Locksley,' said Prince John, 'will you match your skill against Hubert, or yield up to him the prize of the silver bugle-horn?'

'The target is scarcely worth the shooting at,' replied Robin, 'but I will try my fortune – on condition that when I have shot two shafts at yonder mark of Hubert's, he shall be bound to shoot one at whatever mark I may propose.'

'That is but fair,' answered Prince John, 'and it shall be so. Harken, Hubert, if you but beat this braggart, I will fill the bugle-horn with silver pennies for you!'

'A man can but do his best,' said Hubert stolidly, 'but my grandfather drew a good longbow at Hastings, and I trust not to dishonour his memory.'

'Many a good bow was drawn on Senlac Field,' answered Robin, giving the battle its Saxon name. 'But only one side shot their arrows at random into the air: and it was such an arrow that struck King Harold in the eye.'

Prince John flushed angrily at the taunt. 'Impudent braggart!' he exclaimed. 'If you do not justify your boast by mastering Hubert here, you shall be stripped of your Lincoln green and scourged out of the lists with bowstrings as a boaster and a liar!'

'This is no fair match you propose,' said Robin. 'Nevertheless I will risk my skin in it. . . . Do you shoot first, friend Hubert.'

Thus urged, Hubert waited only until a fresh target was set up to discharge his arrow, which landed in the gold but a little to one side.

'You have not allowed for the wind, Hubert,' said Robin, 'or that had been a better shot!' As he spoke he himself loosed an arrow, and although he seemed scarcely to have taken the trouble even to look at the target, his arrow was found to have struck the gold an inch nearer to the white dot in the centre than Hubert's.

'By Heaven!' exclaimed Prince John angrily, 'if you let this runagate knave overcome you, you are worthy of the gallows!'

'Even if your Highness were to hang me,' answered Hubert doggedly, 'I can do no more than my best. Nevertheless, my grandfather drew a good bow –'

'The fiend take your grandfather!' interrupted Prince John. 'Shoot man, and shoot your best, or it shall be the worse for you!'

Thus encouraged Hubert set another arrow to his string, and taking the light breeze into account this time aimed so well that his shaft struck the target exactly in the centre.

'A Hubert! A Hubert!' shouted the onlookers, over-joyed to see a local man fare so well. 'In the dot it is! Hubert wins!'

'You cannot do better than that – Locksley!' sneered Prince John insultingly.

'I will notch his shaft for him, however,' replied Robin, and letting his arrow fly, this time with a little more care, it struck right upon that of his competitor, which it split to shivers.

'And now, your Highness,' said Robin quietly, while the crowd gasped at the shot, and Prince John gnawed his moustache with silent rage, 'I crave permission to plant such a mark as we use in Sherwood!'

With that Robin walked to the nearest thicket and returned with a willow wand about six feet long, per-fectly straight, and not much thicker than a man's thumb. This he peeled, remarking as he did that it was an insult to ask such a fine archer as Hubert to shoot at a target which might just as well be a haystack in a farmer's field.

'But,' he concluded as he went and stuck the willow wand in the ground and returned to Prince John, 'he that hits yonder rod at a hundred yards, I call him an archer fit to bear bow and quiver before any king – even before our good Richard of the Lion Heart himself.'

'My grandfather,' exclaimed Hubert indignantly, 'drew a good bow at the battle of Hastings, but never was he asked to shoot at such a mark in his life, and neither will I. There is no man living who can hit such a target – and if this fellow does so, I'll say he's the devil in person, and willingly yield the prize to him.'

'Cowardly dog!' fumed Prince John. 'Well, Locksley, you split that wand – or by Heaven you smart for it!'

'I will do my best,' answered Robin. 'As Hubert says, no man can do more.'

'Well, Locksley, you have made true your boast'

So saying, he again bent his bow, but on the present occasion looked with care to his weapon, and changed the string, which he thought was no longer truly round, having been a little frayed by his two former shots. He then took his aim very slowly and deliberately, and loosed while the waiting multitude held their breath. The arrow split the willow wand, and a great roar of applause rose from everyone present – and even Prince John could not forbear to say:

'Well, Locksley, you have made true your boast. Here is the silver bugle-horn, and I dare be sworn that no other archer in England could do what you have done. Go in peace now – but remember that I have sworn a certain vengeance, and it shall fall heavily upon the man it concerns, in whatever name he may dress himself.'

Robin bowed in silence, and taking the bugle-horn slipped it into his pouch and mingled quickly with the crowd.

Prince John, already repenting of his generosity, turned to Sir Brian of Bois-Guilbert who sat behind him, and said:

'Know you that yonder braggart archer was none other than Robin Hood, the famous outlaw of Sherwood Forest?'

'I suspected as much,' answered Sir Brian. 'Is it your royal will that I go after him and make him my prisoner?'

'I do not forbid you to do so,' answered Prince John carefully, 'and certainly I would rather the price set on the head of Robin Hood came to you than to any other man I know. . . .'

Sir Brian waited for no more, but leaving the royal stand he gathered his followers together and rode quietly off into the forest.

But it was not to capture Robin Hood that Sir Brian stole away from Ashby-de-la-Zouche so swiftly. It is told in another place how Sir Wilfred of Ivanhoe came to be his prisoner in Torquilstone Castle and the Lady Rowena also; how Cedric the Saxon escaped from it, changing clothes with Wamba the jester, and how it happened that Robin Hood came to their rescue with

all his men, and the mysterious Black Knight rode out
of the wood once more to their assistance.

After the castle had fallen the Black Knight rode back
a little of the way towards the secret glade with Robin,
and in departing left with him a promise to return again.

'And if any danger threatens you, noble sir,' added
Robin, 'so long as you are in Sherwood, know that I or
any of my men will come at once to your aid if you do
but blow our call upon your bugle. Wind three mots
thus " *Wa-sa-hoa*". See now if you can blow them!'

When the Black Knight had blown the call, he
thanked Robin Hood and rode away into the forest.
Nor was it long before he had need of Robin's help.

For Prince John, suspecting who he was, had sent his
most trusted follower the Baron Fitzurse after him from
Ashby-de-la-Zouche with six men to waylay him in
Sherwood and kill him there.

As the Knight rode on among the trees, with only
Wamba the jester as his companion, the traitors closed
in quietly from either side.

It was Wamba who noticed them first.

'We are keeping dangerous company,' he said.

'How so?' asked the Black Knight.

'I have seen the light flash on armour behind the
bushes,' answered Wamba. 'If our attendants were
honest men they would have followed the path and not
us by stealth.'

'By my faith,' said the Knight, 'I think you speak
wisely,' and he closed his visor as he spoke.

Hardly had he done so when three arrows flew at the
same instant from the suspected spot in the thicket, one
of which glanced off his helmet and two more pattered
harmlessly against his shield.

Without a moment's hesitation the Black Knight set
spurs to his horse and charged in the direction from

which the arrows had come. He was met by six or seven men at arms who ran against him with their lances at full career. Three of the weapons struck against him and splintered with as little effect as if they had been driven against a tower of steel. The Black Knight's eyes seemed to flash fire even through the small slits in his visor. 'What means this?' he cried.

But the men charged him again on every side shouting, 'Die, tyrant!'

'Ha, by St George!' roared the Knight, 'have we traitors here?' and he charged them in his turn, hewing down a man at every stroke.

As those left standing drew back, a knight in full armour charged down on him suddenly from among the trees, and laid his horse dead on the ground.

At the same moment Wamba raised his horn to his lips and blew the call which Robin Hood had taught the Black Knight in his presence.

The traitor knight charged again striving to pin the Black Knight to a tree with his lance, but a lucky stroke from Wamba's sword brought him and his horse to the ground. The unequal battle raged for long, but the Black Knight was beginning to grow weary defending himself from attacks from several sides at once. Then suddenly an arrow flashed in the sunlight and one of his assailants fell dead to the ground. A moment later a band of the outlaws came into sight, headed by Robin Hood and Friar Tuck, and disposed speedily of the remaining attackers who soon lay dead or mortally wounded.

'I thank you, good Robin of Locksley,' said the Black Knight gravely. 'Now I pray you stand back a little way while I speak with this knight who has headed so treacherous an attack against me.'

He bent over Baron Fitzurse and spoke with him in a

low voice for some time; then, as he was unwounded, he bade him rise and depart.

'Come with us, good sir knight,' begged Robin when the Black Knight had thanked him again for his timely aid. 'We would entertain you well.'

'Not this time, good friend,' said the Black Knight. 'But be sure I will seek you out ere long.'

Then he mounted upon Wamba's horse and rode slowly away, the jester walking at his side.

Robin looked after him, deep in thought.

'By our Lady,' he said at last to Friar Tuck, 'it would not surprise me greatly if yonder knight be none other than Richard Cœur de Lion himself!'

CHAPTER TWENTY-ONE

ROBIN HOOD AND THE TALL PALMER

Ah, when the King comes home!
That's music – all the birds of April sing
In those four words for me – the King comes home.
ALFRED NOYES: *Robin Hood (1926)*

THERE were rumours everywhere of King Richard's return, and Prince John full of fury, vexation, and disappointment retired to Nottingham and laid desperate plans with his friend and ally the Sheriff.

There various of his supporters came to visit him, and amongst them was the Bishop of Hereford. John entertained him graciously, supplied him with a certain amount of money, and sent him home to raise a rebellion against King Richard there.

'My lord,' said the Bishop, 'I have but a small company, and the road through Sherwood Forest is beset with outlaws: does not Robin Hood dwell there of whose fame as a robber so much is said and sung up and down the country? My lord, I must claim the protection of an armed troop to see me on my way.'

'Not so,' replied John thoughtfully. 'This Robin Hood grows bolder and bolder it is true – and therefore a small company would slip through unobserved where a great one would certainly be attacked. If he does waylay you, tell him you carry money to help King Richard's cause, and as like as not he'll double what you have and send you on your way. He is in open rebellion against me now.'

So, very fearfully, the Bishop with his company of less than a dozen men, set out along the high road from Nottingham.

The moment he had gone Prince John called for his horse and with a picked band of his most faithful followers set out by more secret paths into Sherwood Forest, guided on his way by a forester, one of the few who had not fallen when Robin Hood shot the fifteen verderers after the death of Will Scarlet.

On the hillside between Nottingham and the edge of the forest a tall palmer sat on his horse as still as a statue watching all who went in and came out of the town. Under his palmer's robe he wore a shirt and leggings of chain mail; on his head under the palmer's hood was a skull-cap of steel, and a great sword hung at his side.

Presently a man, running swiftly, came across the fields and spoke to him for a short time. The palmer listened, and his face grew very grim. Then he spoke a few words to the messenger, who saluted and sped back the way he came.

Soon the Bishop of Hereford with his small cavalcade came slowly up the hill, and the palmer rode forward and saluted him humbly.

'My lord,' he said, 'permit me, I beg, to ride with you through the forest. I hear that there are outlaws about, and I would be safer with a reverent company such as yours than going on alone.'

'You are welcome to ride with us, holy palmer,' answered the Bishop. 'But I fear greatly that my men will afford you small protection should Robin Hood attack us.'

Through the leafy avenues of the forest they went, and about noon came to a long, grassy ride with but few trees scattered about it. Under one of these, not far from the road, half a dozen men, dressed in the rough coats of shepherds, were busy skinning and cutting up a newly-slain deer.

The Bishop rode up to them, full of righteous indignation.

'What are you doing here?' he asked, 'and how dare you kill the King's venison, contrary to the forest laws?'

'We are shepherds,' answered the leader, 'and usually we are with our sheep on the Belvoir pastures. But today we have decided to make merry, and so we have killed this fine fat deer for our dinner!'

'Impudent fellow!' gasped the Bishop. 'You shall smart for this under the King's law! Therefore make haste and come along with me, and you shall go before Prince John – who usually hangs deer-slayers for a first offence!'

'Oh mercy, oh mercy!' cried the shepherd. 'Oh, pardon us I pray! It ill becomes a man of your reverent and merciful profession to take away so many lives.'

'No mercy, no mercy!' replied the Bishop, imitating him. 'No mercy for such as you. Therefore make haste – and I hope that Prince John hangs the lot of you!'

Then the shepherd suddenly drew a horn from under his coat and blew three mots upon it.

And while the Bishop sat gaping in surprise and growing fear, the forest all round gave up stalwart bowmen in Lincoln green who came running to the shepherds, who threw off their coats and showed that they also were dressed as foresters.

'What is your will, good master?' said Little John, bending a little before the leading shepherd.

'Here is the Bishop of Hereford,' replied Robin Hood, throwing off the last of his disguise. 'He proposes to hang us all, and will grant us no mercy.'

'Cut off his head, master,' said Little John, 'and bury
him under this tree!'

'Oh mercy, mercy!' cried the Bishop tumbling off his
horse and kneeling to Robin. 'Oh, have mercy on me!
Had I but known that it was Robin Hood, I'd have
gone some other way!'

'No mercy, no mercy!' answered Robin, imitating
the Bishop in his turn. 'Therefore make haste and come
with me to my dwelling place. Little John, bind his eyes,
and some of you do the like for his followers. And take
up the deer.'

The tall palmer who had sat watching this scene
spoke now for the first time. 'Good Robin Hood,' he
said. 'I am not of this man's party, but rode along with
him for company. Nevertheless I cannot sit by and see a
bishop done to death without raising hand to help him.
I have fought in the Holy Land with King Richard, and
the Crusade was against infidel Saracens and for the
defence of Holy Church.'

'Good Palmer,' answered Robin courteously. 'With
you I have no quarrel. But come with us now, taste of
our hospitality – and be sure that only justice shall be
done. But first will you swear by the Holy Sepulchre for
which you have fought that, if we do not blindfold you,
you will never betray the secret path to my dwelling
place.'

'I swear,' answered the Palmer solemnly, and they
set forth, Robin leading the Bishop's horse on one side
and Little John on the other, 'lest his reverence should
chance to stumble among thieves!'

Meanwhile Maid Marian had been left alone in the
secret glade with only Bettris the wife of George-a-
Greene to keep her company.

They sat before the cave talking and lashing the grey

goose feathers onto arrow-shafts while the morning stole on to noon.

'Robin will soon be back,' said Marian. 'He had news that the Bishop of Hereford would pass through the forest this morning, so we may expect guests for dinner!'

'I hope they will pay well!' laughed Bettris. 'I hope – '

She stopped suddenly and gazed fixedly at the bracken.

'What is it, Bettris?' asked Marian.

'I thought I saw a face there in the ferns!' answered Bettris. 'Yonder! Yes, they are shaking still!'

Even as she spoke the bracken parted and Prince John strode into the glade followed by a small band of armed men.

Swiftly Marian whispered something to Bettris, who went hastily into the cave, and then she turned fearlessly to confront Prince John.

'So here's the tigress in her den!' he cried. 'At last, Marian, after all these years, we meet again – and not to part so speedily as last time. ... Come, there is no escape. Our horses wait beyond the rocks with my good forester who tracked you down at last. Robin Hood is too busy with the good Bishop of Hereford: I made sure of that before I came for you!'

Marian stepped backwards quickly, took a horn from her belt and blew the *Wa-sa-hoa* call on it. Then she snatched up the sword which Bettris had brought her, and stood on the defensive.

'Back, you wild beast!' she exclaimed to Prince John. 'Prince or no prince, this sword is between us, and I can use it as well as any man – to defend myself until Robin comes.'

'Quickly!' cried Prince John to his men. 'Catch hold

of her, and then away! Curse you for your slowness!
If you had caught her quicker she could not have
sounded that horn. Now every moment we delay we are
in danger.'

Two of the men closed in upon Marian, who disarmed
one with a quick turn of her wrist, and then after a few
moments of desperate swordplay laid the other dead on
the ground, while Bettris with a blow of a cudgel almost
worthy of George-a-Green himself, felled the first assail-
ant.

Expert fighter though she was, Marian could not
stand long against five armed men, and although she
wounded one of them seriously, and knocked another's
sword from his hand, she was overpowered at last.

'Now we have her!' said Prince John exultantly.
'Come quickly, my pretty, or we'll have that loose
hound of Huntingdon come barking round our heels for
his bitch!'

Her eyes flashing scorn and loathing, Marian struck
John across the face.

With an angry oath he raised his hand to strike back,
when an arrow whizzed between his thumb and first
finger, cutting him to the bone. Had Robin not just run
nearly half a mile almost as fleetly as one of the Sherwood deer the arrow would have transfixed his hand –
and he might have had to sign Magna Carta by proxy.

John spun round, cursing, to find Robin already half-
way across the glade, his sword drawn in his hand.

'Prince John,' shouted Robin, 'you must be tired of
fighting with women, turn and fight with me instead!'

'At him, you four!' snarled John. 'It is Robin Hood,
the outlaw; a great reward to the man who kills him.
Quick, you curs, he's only one!'

The men charged at Robin, who set his back to an
oak tree and fought like one possessed.

'Get round behind!' shouted John. 'I can't leave the girl – she's dangerous!'

'A princely speech indeed!' sneered Robin, and striking one man to the ground he spun round, jumping back as he did so and engaged the other three.

Prince John flung Marian forcibly to the ground, drew his own sword, and drew stealthily nearer to Robin, waiting for a chance to stab him in the back. But his eyes were fixed so intently on his intended victim that he failed to see several figures in Lincoln green drop quietly from the rocks behind the cave. A moment later and he was seized from behind and held firmly, while the three surviving men at arms, seeing Robin's men, turned suddenly and ran for their lives. But not far; several arrows sped from among the trees on either side laid them dead long before they reached the secret path out of the glade.

'Slay him not, but bind him and place him in the cave,' said Robin to the men who held Prince John. Then he turned anxiously to Marian, but she was already on her feet, shaken but unhurt, while Bettris emerged from the cave armed with bows and arrows – too late to be of any help.

'Now,' said Robin, when order was restored and the Bishop of Hereford with his followers had been brought into the glade and set down on the grass. 'Now we have earned our dinner! Come sit down at my table, my lord Bishop, and you, good Palmer, and let us see what appetites you have.'

'You live well here, friend Robin Hood,' said the Palmer as he watched the preparations for dinner.

'But we earn our keep!' smiled Robin.

'Yet you kill the King's deer,' remarked the palmer.

'In that,' answered Robin, 'I hold that we break no just law. For look you, we are outlaws, and so without the law! But I hold that we were not outlawed lawfully: it was John's doing, and that of his minion the Sheriff of Nottingham. We dwell here to set right the wrong: never yet did we hurt any man knowingly who was honest and true, but only those who – with or without the law on their side – robbed innocent men or oppressed them, or did ought against the honour of a woman. They call me the poor man's friend – for I take from the rich to give to the poor: but never have I taken from true knight or worthy priest who held their vows sacred and strove to live according to Our Lord's teaching. I never harmed husbandmen who tilled the ground, nor shepherd minding his flocks, nor any who got their living by honest labour or by honest skill; but I have indeed made prey of those among the clergy, be they simple priests or bishops in their mitres, who oppress their flock, who cheat and rob and lie and follow the pleasures of this world contrary to their holy calling.

'Come now, good master palmer – we are at least thieves of honour, and you do no dishonour to your own noble calling by dining freely with us. That is, unless you shrink from eating the King's deer?'

'Shrink?' the palmer laughed heartily. 'Why, I count it as my own! Fall to in faith, I am as hungry as if I had walked all the way home from Jerusalem – and as thirsty too!'

When the meal was ended, Robin turned to the Bishop.

'My lord,' he said gravely, 'you have dined with me this day. Come, drink with us to King Richard and his speedy return – and then pay us, and begone.'

'So you charge for your meals?' said the palmer. 'And you drink to the King's return, outlaws though you be!'

'We owe it to the King!' said Robin, answering only the last part of the question. 'For after all, our meal is borrowed from him! ... But never have we forgotten, nor could forget, while our horns ring through merry Sherwood, our loyal toast to our most royal master ... Outlaws, the King!'

'The King – and his return from the Crusade!' cried everyone present, leaping to their feet, cup in hand.

'Now, Bishop,' said Robin curtly. 'Have you money with you?'

'But little,' answered the Bishop nervously. 'Not two hundred pieces. And they are not mine: I carry them to those who fight in the King's quarrel against usurpers and tyrants.'

'Search him, his followers and his baggage,' commanded Robin, and then turning to the palmer with a half smile he said:

'Good sir, have you money with you? All that we collect in this way goes – now that the King's ransom is paid off – to those who are in want, the poor, the oppressed, the widow and the orphan.'

'I know not what I have,' said the palmer. 'Sometimes it is much, sometimes little, sometimes none at all. But search me, and take all you find – and for the sake of your kind heart and open hand, be it what it may, I shall wish it were more.'

'Then, since you say so,' cried Robin, 'not a penny will I touch. But you shall play our game of buffets since you are so mighty and stalwart a man. But first the Bishop shall dance a jig for us, for I see that his money is very much more than he remembered, and will take long to count!'

'I cannot dance!' protested the Bishop, trying to look scandalized, but looking only very much afraid.

'Some of you,' ordered Robin, 'prick him gently in the legs with your arrows. He says he cannot dance, but I think he means he will not!'

'Prick him gently in the legs with your arrows'

'I cannot and will not!' shouted the Bishop. 'Oh, take care! I have a swollen vein in my right leg, and if you prick me there, I shall die!'

'Prick him in the other leg,' said Robin calmly. 'Come, dance!'

And the Bishop was forced to pull up his skirts and dance a jig, whether he would or not, while all the outlaws roared with laughter at his comical fat figure and red angry face – and even the tall palmer joined in their mirth.

'Enough, enough,' panted Robin at last. 'We have had sport enough of this kind. But now for our game of buffets!'

'How is it played?' asked the palmer smiling.

'Quite simple,' said Robin. 'You stand up, and receive one buffet from one of us. And if he fails to knock you down, you may strike him a buffet in return.'

'A fine sport, truly,' said the Palmer, and forthwith he bared a fore-arm that any smith might have been proud of, and stood forward.

'Come, Little John,' said Robin, 'and show this good champion that all the men of mettle are not away Crusading.'

Little John rolled up his sleeve, drew back his arm, and dealt a mighty buffet. The palmer seemed scarcely to notice it; instead, he raised his arm and sent Little John sprawling on the turf.

'By the Rood!' cried Friar Tuck, drawing up his sleeve and revealing an arm like a baron of beef. 'Sinew has failed, but let us see what brawn can do!'

With that he delivered a buffet that might have felled an ox. The palmer swayed a little on his feet.

'Well smitten, Friar!' he said with a smile, and putting more power into his blow this time, he laid the fat

friar on his back, where he lay gasping and shouting to
be hauled onto his feet again.

'So much for the Church militant!' said the palmer,
blowing on his knuckles. 'Have I now paid for my
dinner, good Robin?'

'The last blow pays all,' answered Robin, stepping
forward himself. 'I have bowled over the friar before
now – and stood up to his buffet, too. But I am mortally
afraid of you, you mighty man!'

Then the palmer braced himself for the blow, and
Robin smote with all his might. The palmer rocked
perilously on his feet, but neither fell nor gave ground.

'Now my turn, good king of the Forest!' said the
palmer, and he smote Robin Hood to the ground as if he
had been a nine pin.

'You have the best of us!' laughed Robin when he
had found his feet again. 'By Our Lady, you are the
strongest man that ever I met. ... Say now, good
palmer, will you not doff your habit and come dwell
with us here in the greenwood?'

'It cannot be,' said the palmer, a note of regret in his
voice. 'For I go about the King's business.'

'We do his business here, as I have tried to show you,'
answered Robin, but the palmer only shook his head
and smiled.

'Here is one who goes about the devil's business!' exclaimed Little John at this point, and he handed Robin
a letter which he had just ripped from the lining of the
Bishop's gown.

Robin read it, and his brow grew dark.

'By the Mass!' he exclaimed, 'I am minded to hang
you from the nearest tree, master Bishop!'

'Spare me!' shrieked the Bishop, flinging himself on
the ground. 'I had no choice! See you not by whom that
letter is signed.'

'I see,' answered Robin, 'and that reminds me, we have a prisoner – one who assaults women when no man is by to protect them. Bring him before us, Little John!'

So Prince John was led out of the cave, and set before Robin. But when the tall palmer saw him, he uttered an exclamation, and throwing back his hood he stepped forward and confronted the prisoner.

Prince John looked him in the face once, and then he turned a ghastly colour and fell grovelling on his knees.

'Richard!' he gasped. 'King Richard, my brother – come back to punish me.'

'Loose his bonds,' commanded the King. 'Now, go – swiftly – and sin no more!'

Prince John staggered to his feet, reeling and ghastly pale. His horse was brought to him, he clambered upon it, and galloped wildly away.

When he was out of sight, King Richard turned back to Robin Hood, who knelt down before him – an example which was speedily followed by all the outlaws, so soon as the whisper had gone round of 'It is the King.'

'Pardon, my liege,' said Robin.

'Stand up again,' said the King, raising Robin. 'Stand up, my friend – I freely pardon you, and all here present. . . . Except for his grace of Hereford. Robin, I have heard said – for you and your doings are spoken of throughout England – that the Lady Marian lives still a maid until I, the King, return to give her hand to you in marriage. Is this true?'

'It is, my liege,' answered Robin, and Marian came and stood beside him and slipped her hand into his.

'Then here and now I give her to you,' said the King. 'My lord of Hereford shall join your hands in holy matrimony, with Friar Tuck to act as clerk for him. And that good deed shall wipe out what is past. Bishop, perform your office, and then back to your own place and meddle no more in treason.'

So Robin Hood and Maid Marian were wedded there in Sherwood Forest, with Richard Cœur de Lion to give the bride away. And after that they set forward for Nottingham in triumph, Richard riding at the head of them all, with Marian at his side and Robin beyond her.

'My Lord of Huntingdon,' said Richard as they rode, 'your lands and titles are restored to you this day – but I will take from you all those of your late followers who will serve me faithfully. England has many foes, and strong arms and true hearts are needed before we have peace indeed.'

They came into Nottingham like a triumphal procession after a great victory: the ploughman left his plough in the field and ran to see the show, the smith let the iron grow cold upon his anvil, and the aged and infirm rose from their beds and hobbled to their doors to cheer for 'King Richard! King Richard and Robin Hood!'

But the Sheriff fled away in haste, and was not seen again in Nottingham while King Richard was there.

CHAPTER TWENTY-TWO

KING JOHN'S REVENGE

Come, pick the mortar out,
Out of the walls of towers and shrines and tombs.
For now Prince John is King, and Lady Marian
In peril.
ALFRED NOYES: *Robin Hood* (1926)

WITH King Richard's return and the pardon of Robin Hood and all his followers ended the great days in Sherwood Forest.

Robin and Marian lived quietly at Locksley, and there remained with them scarcely a dozen of their old followers, though amongst these was Little John. Friar Tuck also spent much of his time with them, but his real home was again in the Hermit's Cell at Copmanhurst.

King Richard did not remain long in England, but was soon away to the wars again, this time fighting for his own lands in Normandy. With him went the pick of Robin's band to serve as soldiers, and their days in Sherwood were soon forgotten, or remembered only in the songs which the minstrels were already singing of Robin Hood and his Merry Men.

Prince John, pardoned for his treacherous practices against the King, made no attempt to trouble Robin in any way or to renew his attentions to Marian. But very quietly he increased his power and gathered more and more followers – mainly in the north of England. The Sheriff of Nottingham was among these, and he slipped quietly back into power after King Richard had gone, though he too appeared to have forgotten and forgiven all that Robin had done against him.

Five happy years slipped by all too quickly for Robin and Marian, and they paid little attention to the rumours which began to float about. Little John, however, took more heed of what was going on, and more than once he warned Robin.

'Richard has been away for a long time,' he said, 'and John is a man who never forgets or forgives an injury. And remember that were Richard to die, John will be King.'

Robin laughed and shrugged his shoulders.

'I have a full and lawful pardon,' he said. 'John would not – he could not – move against me without fresh cause of offence: and that, since King Richard has so altered the forest laws, I have been careful not to give him.'

'There are rumours that King Richard is dead,' continued Little John. 'Rumours of wars and rebellions – rumours of Prince John being in Nottingham with our old friend the Sheriff.'

'Rumours!' exclaimed Robin impatiently. 'You are full of rumours, Little John – there have been so many rumours, and all of them false. Well, I go into Nottingham this day, and will find out the truth: it is a month since I was last at church, and I would go to mass.'

'Then,' said Little John, 'take a good company with you. Six men at arms at least, leaving another six here to guard the lady Marian.'

Robin laughed. 'Little John, you are still living in our old Sherwood days,' he said. 'You forget that I am again the Earl of Huntingdon – even if but in name – ; you forget certainly that I am the lord of Locksley, and no longer Robin Hood the outlaw!'

'I forget nothing,' said Little John doggedly. 'I only

know that I smell danger – and will not let you run into it alone if I can prevent it.'

'I pray you, dear Robin, do what Little John wishes!' begged Marian.

But Robin shook his head. 'If there *is* danger,' he answered, 'that danger will threaten you rather than me – if it comes from Prince John. Therefore all our men must stay here to guard you, with Little John in command.'

Then Robin kissed Marian, girded on his sword, mounted his horse and rode away to Nottingham.

But Marian turned to Little John.

'Oh, John!' she sobbed. 'I am suddenly afraid! May be it was your words, but I feel suddenly as if Robin were riding out of my life. Go after him, Little John, but do not let him see you: if danger threatens, surely there are many still who would stand by Robin Hood if his bugle-horn rang once more through Sherwood.'

Little John nodded, took his bow, slung a quiver of arrows over his back, and set forth on foot through the forest paths.

'Alas!' sighed Marian, looking round the comfortable room and out at the trim garden of Locksley Hall, 'I fear that the good days are ending!'

Robin rode quietly into Nottingham and put up his horse at an inn. Then he walked through the streets to St Mary's Church: he felt as he went that there was an air of suspense and excitement, but there was no sign of anything being out of the ordinary.

'I will ask questions presently,' he thought to himself as he brushed past a tall monk at the entrance to the church. Then he put all worldly thoughts from his mind as he knelt before the altar while the priest proffered the Holy Sacrament to him.

But the monk who had passed him in the doorway went at full speed to the Sheriff's house.

'Rise up, rise up, master Sheriff!' he exclaimed.
'Robin Hood, alone and unarmed, has even now gone
into St Mary's Church!'

'Come with me!' cried the Sheriff eagerly, and together they went to the Castle, where John had arrived
the previous night.

'Robert of Locksley is in Nottingham, your Majesty,'
said the Sheriff, bowing very low. 'He does not know of
Richard's death, otherwise he would not be here.'

'It is not known anywhere yet,' said King John,
'unless you have disobeyed my orders and proclaimed
it – which I would not have until tomorrow. . . . But this
is truly good news. Go you, master Sheriff, with as many
of my men as you think needful, and bring him here.
You need have no fear – my men are all mercenaries,
hired abroad: they will obey without question. And
while you are away, I will make ready for him!'

Off went the Sheriff with a dozen men at arms, and
came to St Mary's Church. And when Robin came out
after Mass, his eyes cast down and thinking still of the
goodness of God rather than of the sinfulness of men,
they seized him before he had time even to draw his sword.

'What means this outrage, master Sheriff?' asked
Robin indignantly, recognizing his old enemy. 'I am a
free man, and owe my allegiance to the King alone.'

'It is by the King's orders that I come for you, my
lord of Huntingdon,' answered the Sheriff, anxious to
avoid attracting attention. 'He has come secretly to
Nottingham and bade me fetch you before him, hearing
things charged against you – of which doubtless you can
acquit yourself.'

So Robin came peacefully into Nottingham Castle,
and followed the Sheriff up the steep spiral staircase in
the keep. But as they went higher and higher, he began
to have grave doubts.

'Whither do you take me?' he asked.

'To the King,' answered the Sheriff as before.

'He surely does not hold court in a turret top,' exclaimed Robin.

'You forget that he has come here in secret,' answered the Sheriff readily enough. They came at last to the top of the stair and so into a room of some size immediately under the roof. In one corner was a narrow doorway leading to a chamber about six feet across, formed by the top of the turret at the next corner, and four men with masons' tools were building up the doorway.

'So we meet again, Robin Hood!' said a smooth, cruel voice.

'If you mean any ill towards me, Prince John,' answered Robin, 'I bid you beware! King Richard will not lightly forgive you a second time if you fall again into treason.'

The Sheriff struck Robin across the face.

'Mind your evil tongue, you dog!' he cried exultantly. 'You speak to the King now!'

'The King!' gasped Robin.

'Yes,' said John quietly. 'Richard my brother lies dead in Normandy: the news was brought to me not two days since – and I have kept it secret as yet, the better to entrap certain traitors such as you.'

Robin looked at John steadily for a minute, and then turned away.

'This is a cruel and a mean revenge,' he said. 'I wonder that a King can stoop to it, or even think that it is worth the sin upon his soul to seek it.'

'Ah,' said John, 'but when you are dead there will be no one to stand between me and Lady Marian – as you stood that day in Sherwood Forest. When you are dead? Before you are dead! For see how merciful I am: you are not to die this night, nor indeed will I or our good

friend the Sheriff permit you to be slain. But you see
yonder the place prepared for you: there, good, just
outlaw, you may kneel and pray – for death. When that
wall is built up, with the great door locked in case of
accidents, even your voice will not be heard again. A
window? There is a window indeed, and were the bar
out of it, a man might clamber through the space and
hurl himself to death. . . . Well, we must chance that –
but self slaughter, let me remind you, my pious friend,
is a deadly sin. So, fling him in. That's it, the rope to the
ring in the wall. . . . By the time you slip that rope,
friend Robin, the mortar will be hard that walls you up
– and I will be at Locksley with lovely Marian!'

'Devil!' gasped Robin. 'Alas, poor England, ruled by
such a king as you!'

Then, while Robin strained in vain at the rope which
held him to the ring in the wall of the little turret room,
the masons built up the wall – a good three feet of solid
stone – and until the last chink was stopped King John
did not cease to taunt Robin and boast of how he would
carry off Marian from Locksley that very night.

Left alone in the cell which was like to be his tomb,
Robin, grown calmer, worked away desperately but
more carefully at the rope which bound him. When at
last he was free of this, his first thought was for the doorway. But even a rough glance told him that escape that
way was hopeless.

So he turned his attention to the narrow window, and
found that the one bar down its centre was rusted a little,
though firmly set in the masonry at top and bottom.
Seizing it by the middle, Robin put his feet against the
wall and strained with all his might. Slowly, very slowly
the iron bent, until at last it slipped out of its socket
and Robin fell back upon the floor with it upon him.

Rising hastily he clambered up into the narrow window place and gazed out. The sun was setting red and angry over Sherwood and shining upon him. Below, the castle lay in shadow; below – so far below that he shuddered as he looked – lay the castle garden, a hundred feet or more beneath him, with smooth stone all the way.

It seemed hopeless, but Robin felt in his pouch which had not been taken from him and drew out the silver bugle-horn he had won at Ashby-de-la-Zouche. Leaning out of the window he raised it to his lips and blew the old familiar call. Then he drew back lest any in the castle should see him, and listened.

A moment later his call was answered from nearby, and by the note he knew that it was blown by Little John.

Robin took off his shirt, fastened it to the iron bar, hung it from the window, and drawing back into the cell, waited patiently.

Nearly an hour later, when the light was gone, an arrow came suddenly through the window and fell upon the stone floor.

Eagerly Robin picked it up, to find, as he had hoped, a thin thread fastened to it. Slowly and carefully he drew the thread through the window, yards and yards of it. Presently the thread brought him the end of a thin cord, and this in turn was fastened to a rope of sufficient thickness to bear him.

Swiftly he tied the rope to the ring in the wall, and then, after a short prayer, slid feet first out of the window and climbed slowly and carefully down, down towards the ground so far beneath.

It was a terrifying descent, for the rope was thin and Robin swayed perilously from side to side. Moreover he knew that sooner or later the rope would fray through

An arrow came suddenly through the window

where it was stretched over the rough sill of the prison window. This indeed happened when he was some twenty feet from the ground, and Robin fell, and lay insensible for a while.

When he recovered Little John was bending over him. Robin staggered to his feet, whole in his limbs, but with a burning pain that told of some internal hurt caused by the fall.

'Quickly, come quickly, dear master,' whispered Little John. 'There is a secret way out, and two horses await us beyond the walls.'

'We must hasten to Locksley!' gasped Robin.

Little John nodded. 'John and the Sheriff with twenty men at arms rode out of the castle half an hour since,' he said. 'Thanks be to Reynolde Greenleafe who was our man in Sherwood and now commands the castle guard, I discovered where you were. He knew nothing of it, but got at the truth from one of these foreign fellows whom John brings here because he fears his own countrymen. Reynolde learnt too that they ride to Locksley. When he knew all, he let me into this garden and showed me how we might go unseen out of the castle. He sent a message also to Much who now owns the mill on the high road – the horses that wait us are his.'

Together, with Little John supporting Robin, they threaded their way by dark passages from the castle and out into the Forest. There the two horses were awaiting them, tied to a tree, and they had but to mount and ride.

The angry sunset had been followed by wind and fierce squalls of rain, and the riders bent low upon their horses' necks as they galloped by the paths which Robin knew so well.

They came to Locksley Hall before King John and his men, but only by a few minutes.

'We cannot defend this house,' gasped Robin. 'My
honest friends, get you gone swiftly. Marian, to horse
and away: King John and the Sheriff are without and
more than twenty men at arms accompany them.'

Then some of Robin's men slipped away as he had
bidden them, but others saddled horses, looked to their
weapons, and vowed they would die by Robin's side.

Ten minutes later they rode out into the night, Robin
Hood, Marian, and Little John, with four followers.
Their enemies had surrounded the place, and the moon
shining fitfully between the clouds flashed back from
armour and drawn swords.

'Ride north,' directed Robin. 'Onto the Great North
Road. Ready now, charge them at full gallop – it is our
only hope.'

The little cavalcade set spurs to their horses and
charged their attackers, who massed together to receive
them. The moon shone brightly at that moment, and
Robin found the Sheriff of Nottingham in front of
him.

'It is the ghost of Robin Hood!' screamed the Sheriff,
a ghastly green in the moonlight. Then Robin's sword
passed through him, and he fell and writhed upon the
ground and died.

Two of Robin's men fell in that encounter, but the
rest of them broke through and galloped away.

Then began a long, long chase through the night.
The King's men gained very little, but Robin could
never shake them off. Once Marian's horse caught its
foot and went lame. One of the two remaining followers
gave her his horse, and with a word of farewell slipped
away into the forest through which they were riding.

Once two of King John's men outstripped the rest and
came perilously near. Then the other follower, with no
order from Robin, turned suddenly and charged the

men, and slew both of them but was himself slain by the rest of the mercenaries.

Towards morning, somewhat in advance of their pursuers, Robin halted suddenly at a side road.

'A mile down there,' he gasped, 'lies the Nunnery of Kirkleys. John, do you take Marian thither and let her seek sanctuary of the Prioress, who is a most holy woman and will not break sanctuary even for the King.'

'I go not without you!' cried Marian. 'Come to sanctuary also, Robin!'

'You may be safe there,' said Robin, 'but not I. Go, Marian, if you love me. And you too, John: it is my last command. If I live, I will seek you there. But I fear that I am a dead man. That fall when the rope gave has torn something inside me. I do not think I could walk many paces – but I can still lead John and his men a good chase. One kiss, sweet Marian, and then farewell – perhaps for ever in this world.'

Then they clung and kissed, and after a brief moment Marian and Little John rode away towards Kirkleys. They were scarcely out of sight when the first of King John's men came into view and saw Robin.

Then Robin bent once more over his horse's neck, clapped spurs into its side, and rode on into the morning.

CHAPTER TWENTY-THREE

ROBIN HOOD'S LAST ADVENTURE

*Now quoth Robin, I'll to Scarborough go
That I a fisherman brave may be!*
- BALLAD: *The Noble Fisherman.*

WHEN he parted from Marian and Little John, Robin Hood rode northwards for only a little distance, and then turned towards the east, hoping to throw off the pursuit. But King John's men were after him still, and chased him over the bleak Yorkshire moors until they came down the long slopes into Scarborough and saw the sun rising out of the grey sea.

Robin clattered over the cobbles of the little fishing town, sprang off his horse at the first inn he came to – and then stumbled away down a side street in the direction of the harbour. A few minutes later his pursuers arrived, saw his horse, and in a moment were overrunning the inn to find him.

Meanwhile, Robin stumbling with pain and weariness found a house on the quayside where lodgings were to be let to seamen. And there the widow woman who was his hostess welcomed him kindly and set food before him.

'I am a poor fisherman,' said Robin, in answer to her questions, 'and I have travelled across the country from Helsby in Cheshire. . . . My name is Simon Lee. . . . On the way I fell in with lawless men who robbed me of all I had, and pursued me to this very place.'

All that day Robin rested at the widow's house, and

in the evening walked out through the streets, leaning on a stick. Very soon he found that all the gates were guarded, and all those going in or out were stopped and questioned.

Robin sat on the quayside and gazed out over the twilit sea, wondering what to do. There were several people to whom he might turn for help, such as Sir Richard of Legh or Allin-a-Dale: but he knew that sooner or later King John's agents would find him out, and then his friends would suffer for sheltering him.

'I cannot even escape to Wakefield and take service with George-a-Greene,' thought Robin, 'nor return to Sherwood either as a shepherd with Lionel and Eglamour or to gather a fresh band of outlawed men about me. . . .'

Robin returned sadly to his lodgings, and here the way of escape was waiting for him.

'Good fisherman Simon,' said the widow as she set his supper before him. 'You tell me that you have but two pieces of gold in the world, and that you seek for employment? Will you not then be my man, and I'll promise you a good wage? For I have a ship of my own as good as any that sails the sea. Tomorrow at the first light it sails from the quay yonder, and there lacks from the crew yet one fisherman.'

'Right willingly will I serve you,' said Robin thankfully, and by the next morning he had stepped aboard the ship and was sailing out into the North Sea.

They sailed on for several days, and then cast anchor on a sandbank while the fishermen prepared their nets, and lines, and cast them into the sea. But Robin, who knew nothing of sea-fishing, cast in his lines unbaited, and caught no fish.

Then the captain jeered at him. 'It will be long indeed before this great lubber does well at sea!' he cried. 'Well, I can promise him that he shall have no share in our gains when this voyage is ended – for he has not earned so much as a penny piece!'

'Now woe is me!' exclaimed Robin. 'If I were but in Plompton Park I could bring in the red deer fast enough. Here every clown laughs me to scorn because I cannot catch fish: but if I had them in the forest, they would do little enough good there, I'll warrant!'

They sailed on for many days after this, and at length one day, Robin espied a ship of war bearing down upon them.

'Now woe is me!' cried the captain in his turn. 'Here comes a French pirate craft to take all our fish from us, and may be sell us into slavery as well, or cast us into the sea. They will not spare one man of us; but what can we do to escape them? Nothing, nothing! Alas and woe the day!'

'Do not despair!' cried Robin. 'Good captain, all will yet be well. Give me but my long-bow and a good quiver of arrows, and I will not spare one of these sea robbers!'

'Hold your peace, you long lubber Simon!' snapped the captain. 'You are nought but brags and boasts. If I should cast you overboard, you would be no great loss!'

Nevertheless, as neither the captain nor the rest of the crew showed any signs of trying to defend themselves, Robin seized his bow, and having tied himself to the mast so as to be steady on his feet, set an arrow on the string, loosed, and laid the pirate captain dead on his own quarter-deck. Then, as the two ships drew closer and closer together, Robin loosed arrow after arrow, and at each shot a man fell from the rigging or crumpled up on the deck.

Presently the two ships were alongside one another.

'Now, captain!' cried Robin, loosing himself from the

mast. 'Follow me, and follow men, one and all. The ship is ours, there is nothing to fear!'

So saying, he boarded the pirate craft, followed by all the seamen, and easily overpowered the few pirates who had escaped his arrows.

Robin laid the pirate captain dead on his own quarter-deck

When the brief battle was ended and the prisoners securely tied, Robin and the captain searched their prize, and found more than twelve thousand pounds worth of gold, besides many other treasures.

'By the Rood, good Simon,' said the captain. 'I misjudged you grossly. Truly men do ill to jeer at any who cannot do what they can do themselves – for ever it seems that there is something which they can do better. Were it not for you and your skill with the bow, we would all have been prisoners, or dead men, by now. And therefore I say that all this treasure belongs to you.'

'Why then,' said Robin, 'half of it all belongs by right to the good widow whose ship we sail in, and to her orphaned children. As for the other half, let us share that amongst ourselves.'

But the captain still insisted that it was his.

'Good Simon Lee,' he said, 'the widow will reward us well, that I am certain. Therefore take the rest which is most assuredly yours.'

Then Robin filled his pouch with gold, and handed the rest to the captain saying:

'Good sir, I need only what I can carry with me. Let us now hasten back to England with our prize. And do you take the rest of my share to Scarborough and there build almshouses for the poor. But first of all set me ashore in some quiet bay on the coast of Yorkshire, for I have enemies that may await me in Scarborough.'

So they sailed back to England, and one night dropped anchor in the cove which has ever since been known as Robin Hood's Bay.

'Fare well, brave Simon Lee,' said the captain as Robin stepped ashore with his bow and quiver on his back, and a stout staff in his hands.

'Fare well, captain,' was the answer, 'and if any ask who was the fisherman who could not fish, yet brought to land a richer haul than any of you, say that his name was not Simon Lee, but Robert of Huntingdon, whom men call Robin Hood!'

So saying Robin turned and limped away into the darkness while the captain and the seamen gazed after him with open mouths.

CHAPTER TWENTY-FOUR

THE LAST ARROW

Weep, weep, ye woodmen, wail,
Your hands with sorrow wring;
Your master Robin Hood lies dead,
Therefore sigh as you sing.

Here lie his primer and his beads,
His bent bow and his arrows keen,
His good sword and his holy cross:
Now cast on flowers fresh and green.

ANTHONY MUNDAY: *The Death of Robert*
Earl of Huntingdon (1601)

AT Kirkleys Nunnery the Prioress welcomed Marian
and led her at once to sanctuary, while Little John
turned hastily away and lay waiting in the woods.

Several days later King John's men came to the
Nunnery demanding that Marian should be given up to
them.

But the Prioress refused. 'The Lady Marian has taken
sanctuary,' she said, 'and not the King himself can
touch her now. I have no love for Robin Hood, but
were it he and not his wife who knelt with hand on the
altar, he were yet inviolate.'

And so she answered all messengers who came,
whether they threatened or pleaded or sought to bribe
her.

But when they had gone she spoke with Marian many
times.

'Good daughter,' she said, 'I have certain news that
Robin Hood is dead. Moreover, though I will withstand

him to the last, King John may yet take you hence by
force. But if you once vow yourself to God, take the veil
and become one of our sisterhood, then you are safe
indeed. Were John twenty times a king, all England
would rise and put him from the throne did he violate
a Nunnery and tear a nun from the altar.'

So the Prioress persuaded Marian until Marian
believed indeed that Robin was dead. And if this were
so, she asked nothing better than to take the veil and
pass the rest of her days in prayer to God and in tending
upon the sick.

But the Prioress had other reasons besides those she
had given for urging Marian to become a nun. For she
knew that Marian was the heir to all the Locksley
estates, and, Robin, being dead, if Marian became a
member of Kirkleys, all that she owned became the
property of the Nunnery also.

At long last the Prioress had her way, and Marian
became a nun: but only after King John had himself
come to the Nunnery and demanded her in person.
Then Marian hesitated no longer, and John turned
away in baffled fury, for as the Prioress had said even he
dared not tear a nun from a Nunnery – and he was not
yet prepared to defy the Pope and his Interdict.

'Look you, mother Prioress,' he said before he went
away. 'This proscribed traitor and thief, Robin Hood,
may still be alive: no one has seen him for many months,
but I cannot again believe him dead until I, or trustworthy witnesses, have seen his body laid in the grave.
If he lives, he who is an enemy to the Church may come
here and take Marian away from you: and mark me
well, if Marian leaves you to go to Robin Hood, then
I will burn your Nunnery to the ground and turn you
and your nuns out into the world to starve.'

Then he laughed savagely and rode away. But the

Prioress set guards round the Nunnery and throughout her lands and estates, for the last thing she wished was for Robin Hood's return. But she did not know that one of the lay brothers who served without the Nunnery gates was Little John.

At long last Robin Hood came. He came leaning on a stick, an old, sick man, though he was not much more than forty, for he had never recovered from the fall when the rope broke as he climbed down out of King John's prison cell. He had limped his way painfully across country to Kirkleys, growing rapidly iller and weaker as he went, and now he knocked at the door and begged the Prioress's aid.

'Come in, good sir,' said the Prioress gently, and she led him to the guest chamber, a room on the ground floor that looked out towards Sherwood. Then she put Robin to bed, and opened a vein in his arm to let blood, which was considered at that time to be one of the most certain cures for all illnesses.

Presently Robin recovered a little and sat up.

'Good Mother Prioress,' he said. 'I may speak to you under the seal of confessional, may I not, knowing that nothing I tell you will be heard outside these walls?'

'Speak on, son,' answered the Prioress, 'and besides myself God alone shall hear what you tell me.'

'Then know,' said Robin, 'that I am Robert Fitzooth, formerly Earl of Huntingdon, who am known as Robin Hood.'

The Prioress stirred suddenly, but said nothing, and Robin went on:

'Good mother Prioress, many months ago my wife Marian and I fled from Nottingham, pursued by King John and his men. When I knew that we could not escape together, I sent Marian to take sanctuary here while I led our pursuers on towards Scarborough. Mother Prioress, what news have you for me of my wife?'

'She came here,' answered the Prioress, very pale, but speaking quietly. 'And here she stayed for a little while. Then she rode away again, I think to your hall at Locksley, there to await you.'

'Then there I must seek her!' cried Robin, trying to rise from the bed.

'When you are better,' said the Prioress. 'Sleep now, and tomorrow may be you can travel. Then I will lend you a horse, and two of my serving men shall ride with you.'

Then Robin lay back on the bed and slept, for he was very weak. But as soon as she was certain he was sleeping, the Prioress loosened the bandage from his arm so that the blood flowed once more. Then she stole quietly away and left him.

All day Robin lay there bleeding slowly to death, and when the shadows were lengthening he awoke and looked about him. He was so weak now that he could scarcely move, but he saw that the bandage had been unfastened purposely, and he guessed that the Prioress had done it.

Robin staggered to his feet and flung open the windows. It was but a short drop to the ground, and beyond the garden he saw the forest, his forest, beckoning to him. But he could not so much as raise his leg to climb over the window sill.

Then he thought of his bugle-horn. With trembling fingers he drew it from his pouch, raised it to his lips and blew the old call *Wa-sa-hoa* for the last time.

Out in the forest Little John heard it.

'That was Robin's horn!' he exclaimed. 'But I fear my master is near to death, he blows so wearily!'

Then he hastened to the Nunnery, with several of the lay brothers following him. And when they would not let him in, he seized a great hammer and broke the locks on every door that stood in his way.

But another had heard the bugle call. Marian the nun knelt in the chapel praying for the soul of her dead husband when the notes came to her ears from nearby.

Then she sprang to her feet, hope and fear in her eyes, and followed the echoes of that call until she came to the guest chamber and found Robin lying back exhausted on the bed.

'Oh, Robin, my lord, my love!' she cried, and Robin's arms sought to hold her and draw her to him, but could not.

'Marian,' he whispered. 'They told me you were far away at Locksley!'

Then very shortly Marian told him what had happened, and he told her of his adventures.

'Here have I come to die,' he said, 'and where else could I ask to die but in your arms.'

By this time Little John had broken into the room, and now he knelt weeping at Robin's side.

'Oh, my master, my master,' he sobbed. 'Grant me one last boon! This evil Prioress has slain you – and cheated your Lady Marian. Let me burn Kirkleys Nunnery and slay this wicked woman!'

'Not so,' answered Robin. 'That is a boon I will not grant you. Never in my life did I hurt a woman nor raise my hand against a maid, nor shall it be done at my death. Do not blame the lady Prioress, for my death was upon me, as I have known for long. But give me my bent bow and set a broad arrow on the string, and where the arrow falls, there bury me. Lay a green sod under my head and another at my feet, and lay my bent bow at my side which was sweet music while I lived. Then

'Give me my bent bow and set a broad arrow on the string,
and where the arrow falls, there bury me'

cover me with the green turf of the forest and set a stone
at my head so that all men may know where Robin
Hood of Sherwood lies buried.'

Then, weeping bitterly, Little John placed the bow
in Robin's hand and guided his fingers to the notched
arrow. For the last time Robin Hood drew his good yew
bow, and as he drew strength seemed to come to him so
that he drew the arrow to the very head and loosed it so
strongly that it flew well beyond the Nunnery walls and
fell in a deep green glade of the forest.

Then Robin Hood fell back into Little John's arms,
and Marian closed his eyes and wept over her dead
lord.

But next morning Little John sought out the arrow, and where it fell he dug Robin's grave with his own hands, and laid him to rest under the greenwood tree. And at his head he set a stone, and on it, when the first inscription had worn away, these lines were cut:

> *Underneath this little stone*
> *Lies Robert Earl of Huntingdon;*
> *No other archer was so good –*
> *And people called him Robin Hood.*
> *Such outlaws as he and his men*
> *Will England never see again.*

KING HENRY AND THE HERMITS

And yet I think these oaks at dawn and even
Will whisper ever more of Robin Hood . . .
. . . You, good Friar,
You Much, you Scarlet, you dear Little John,
Your names will cling like ivy to the wood.
And here perhaps a hundred years away
Some hunter in day-dreams or half asleep
Will hear our arrows whizzing overhead,
And catch the winding of a phantom horn.

TENNYSON: *The Foresters (1881)*

AFTER Robin Hood's death, Marian dwelt on in Kirk-leys Nunnery where she soon became Prioress under the name of Matilda. And of the goodness of the Prioress Matilda and of how she was ever ready to help the sick and the afflicted many tales were told. At the last she died in the room where Robin had died, and was buried beside him under the greenwood tree.

Little John, however, did not stay at Kirkleys after he had laid his beloved friend and master in the grave. For some years he dwelt in Ireland, where his feats of archery are still remembered; then he returned to England and was no more heard of, though his grave is still shown at Hathersage in Derbyshire.

There is a story, however, that long after King John's death his son King Henry III hunted the deer in Sherwood Forest. And there he started the finest stag that ever a man hunted, and pursued it so fast and so far that as night came on he found himself separated from his followers and lost in the wildest parts of the forest.

Wandering in search of a night's lodging he came at length to a well-worn path, and following it found himself at a little chapel by which stood a hermit's cell. There was a light in the chapel and entering the King found two hermits at their prayers, two very old men, one tall beyond the ordinary and the other broad and fat even in age.

The two hermits seemed very loath to entertain the wanderer, and when at last they let him enter their cell, gave him a truss of straw to lie upon and regretted that they had no supper to offer him but bread and cheese and to drink only the water from a nearby spring.

'Surely,' said the King, 'with the forest all about you, you could fare better than this? Come now, do you never draw a bow when the verderers are asleep?'

'Alas, we are poor men,' said the tall hermit, 'I fear that you seek to entrap us by forcing a confession that we have broken the forest laws.'

'Never would I betray the man who gave me a good square meal tonight,' said the King, 'for never have I needed it more!'

Presently the King bethought him of the flask of strong old wine that hung at his saddle, and after a little persuasion the fat hermit consented to drink of it with him and speedily grew merry.

Then one thing led to another and the two hermits brought out wine and ale of their own, and presently the board was heaped with venison pasties and delicacies of all sorts.

'Can you draw a good bow, sir huntsman?' asked the tall hermit presently, and upon the King saying that he could the three of them went out into the twilight and tried their skill at a willow wand set up at thirty yards distance. But only the tall hermit could split it.

Later as they sat drinking the King exclaimed:

'Never have I seen such archery nor been so well entertained in the forest. I could almost believe that we were back in the days of King Richard of the Lion Heart when bold Robin Hood ruled in the Forest of Sherwood of whom so many songs are sung and so many tales are told – know you any tales of that king of outlaws, that noble prince of thieves?'

Then the two old hermits seemed to grow young again, and the morning came while they were still telling their guest of all that had chanced in Sherwood so long ago – adventures which they themselves had seen, in which they themselves had played a part.

With the first light the King mounted on his horse once more (albeit unsteadily, for he had drunk deep throughout the night) and rode away in search of his followers. But before he went he turned to his two hosts and said:

'Reverent hermits, if I have not dreamt it, I supped last night in Sherwood Forest with Little John and Friar Tuck!'

When he found his courtiers once more the King told them of his strange adventure, and all marvelled to hear of it. But, though he and they sought long and eagerly, they could never again find their way to that hidden cell in Sherwood Forest.